He could have her now. Kiss her into submission, take her up against the dark, dirty wall of this neglected hallway, and he would swear that she wouldn't even fight him.

And he would have gone that way once. In his youth he wouldn't have thought twice about it. Young and wild, he had operated only on instinct, on hunger, on need. But Katherine Charlton was a very different matter.

He had sensed that hunger in her kiss. In the tiny whimper she had made under his mouth, the way her body had melted against him. And he hadn't even touched her. But one day he would. One day she would leave all her pride in the dust and she would beg for his touch. And the waiting, the anticipation, would only make the fulfillment all the more delicious, more satisfying.

He could wait. And enjoy that anticipation.

Dear Reader,

You'll see this book is partly dedicated to a Mr. Grogan, who first introduced me to the story of *Wuthering Heights.* I was just ten years old, and living just down the road from where the Brontë sisters grew up. One day, to distract us from the heavy storms outside, our teacher started to read us *Wuthering Heights.* We only ever heard the start of the story—up to the moment when Heathcliff turned his back on Cathy and walked away to make his fortune—so I didn't know what happened until I found a copy on my mother's bookshelves and found myself caught up in the story.

I had always hoped that *Wuthering Heights* would have a happy-ever-after for Cathy and Heathcliff. But even from the start I had somehow known that that wasn't going to be—that, whatever else it was, *Wuthering Heights* wasn't really a love story but a story about passion and possession. So when I was asked to rework *Wuthering Heights,* I could take the wild, strong-willed Cathy and the dark, brooding, dangerous Heathcliff and let them learn about love, so as to give them the happy ending Emily Brontë's original story could never have had.

Emily Brontë's *Wuthering Heights* was a vital part of my life right from that day in my childhood, and I still reread the book at least once a year, so writing *The Return of the Stranger* was a dream come true for me. I've loved reworking this classic story, and I hope you'll love the result when you read it.

Kate Walker

www.kate-walker.com

THE RETURN OF
THE STRANGER
KATE WALKER

~ The Powerful and the Pure ~

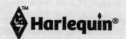

TORONTO NEW YORK LONDON
AMSTERDAM PARIS SYDNEY HAMBURG
STOCKHOLM ATHENS TOKYO MILAN MADRID
PRAGUE WARSAW BUDAPEST AUCKLAND

Recycling programs
for this product may
not exist in your area.

ISBN-13: 978-0-373-52834-9

THE RETURN OF THE STRANGER

First North American Publication 2011

www.Harlequin.com

Printed in U.S.A.

KATE WALKER was born in Nottinghamshire, England, and grew up in a home where books were vitally important. Even before she could write she was making up stories. She can't remember a time when she wasn't scribbling away at something.

But everyone told her that she would never make a living as a writer, so instead she became a librarian. It was at the University College of Wales, Aberystwyth, that she met her husband, who was also studying at the college. They married and eventually moved to Lincolnshire, where she worked as a children's librarian until her son was born.

After three years of being a full-time housewife and mother she was ready for a new challenge, so she turned to her old love of writing. The first two novels she sent off to Harlequin® were rejected, but the third attempt was successful. She can still remember the moment that a letter of acceptance arrived instead of the rejection slip she had been dreading. But the moment she really realized that she was a published writer was when copies of her first book, *The Chalk Line,* arrived just in time to be one of her best Christmas presents ever.

Kate is often asked if she's a romantic person, because she writes romances. Her answer is that if being romantic means caring about other people enough to make that extra special effort for them, then, yes, she is.

Kate loves to hear from her fans. You can contact her through her website at www.kate-walker.com or email her at kate@kate-walker.com.

Books by Kate Walker
Harlequin Presents® EXTRA

146—*THE PROUD WIFE*
122—*THE GOOD GREEK WIFE?*

For my junior school teacher,
Mr. Grogan, who first told me the story of
Wuthering Heights, and
for Michelle Styles, who always believed.
(Not forgetting Heathcliff the Cat!)

CHAPTER ONE

HE WAS back.

Heath stood on the moorland rise that was positioned almost exactly halfway between the two houses that had shaped his life in the past. Up above him, high on the steep hill, was the big old-fashioned stone building known as High Farm. Neglected now, and desperately in need of repair, the window frames crumbling, the garden overgrown, it looked bleak and unwelcoming as the winds lashed the trees behind it. Further down in the valley was the Grange, elegant, well cared for, with sweeping lawns, a flourishing rose garden and there, at the side of the big golden-stoned house, the glint of blue where the swimming pool gleamed in the sunlight.

One of these houses had been the place he had grown up in but had never truly been able to call home. He had spent most of his childhood and adolescence there but he had never belonged. Always been on the outside. And once the man who had brought him there had died, any trace of warmth or 'family' had vanished with him.

The other house he'd been totally excluded from. Not even allowed through the door, never mind into any of the elegant, expensively decorated rooms. Just once he'd crossed the threshold, getting as far as the hall and that was as far as he'd managed. That time he had been ejected with a hand on the collar of his shirt, a knee in his back, thrown out onto the rain-soaked gravel driveway, landing on his face with such force that he had been picking bits of stone out of the grazes for days to come.

He was back but there was no way that he was *home*.

'Home! Hah!'

He kicked a pebble out of his way, watched it bounce along the path then fall into a rough patch of grass. This had never been his home even when he had thought, had hoped that it was. Ten years before, a penniless adolescent, he had turned his back on it without a second thought, driven out by one last betrayal, one last rejection, that had been more than he could take. Heading out into a night so vile it had seemed as if all the devils in hell were howling in the wind that whirled across the moor, and the icy rain had almost blinded him as it swept into his eyes, plastered his hair to his skull.

With only the clothes he stood up in and his paltry savings in his pocket, the amount so small that he would now think more than twice about even tossing it into a beggar's collection pot, he had vowed that one day he would be back. That one day he would return. But not until he had the status, the wealth, the power, that meant that neither the Nicholls family nor the Charltons would ever be able to make a move against him again.

It had taken him ten years, but now he was ready. They said that revenge was a dish best served cold and in those years he had had time to become as cold as ice, and more than ready to make a meal of his vengeance. Already things were set in place, he had played the first card, moved the first domino that would soon have his enemies' every last defence crashing down to the ground.

Once again the blustering wind fretted at his hair, blasting it across his frowning forehead and into his narrowed eyes. As he pushed it back he felt the ridge of the scar that ran along his cheekbone, smiling grimly as he recalled just who had put it there and why.

Before the week was out, Joseph Nicholls would regret that blow—and many more.

And Joseph's sister? What about Kat?

'Katherine…'

Thinking of her had been a mistake. He found that he was shaking his head roughly in an attempt to drive away the memories that simply thinking of her had dragged up from the dark chambers of his mind. Chambers where he had thought that he had buried them for good.

He had things to do; plans to put into action. And he was not about to let the memory of the girl—the woman now—who had once taken what little was left of his heart and trampled it under her feet distract him from his purpose now that his aim was almost achieved. He would see her later of course. How could he come back to Hawden and not come face to face with her? He could never leave without exorcising the bitter legacy she had left him with, the scars that went deeper than the ones on his body, on his face that her brother and her husband had put there.

He would have to see her one last time before he left Hawden Valley for good. But he had other things to do first. Other memories to erase, cruelties and injustices to avenge. He was ready to show the families who had treated him as less than the dirt beneath their feet that they no longer had any power over him. Instead, he was now the one with all the control in his hands.

Katherine Nicholls—Katherine Charlton—could wait a while longer. He had to see her to close the door on what had once been between them and know that everything was now behind him. That would be the last thing he had to do before he could shake the dirt of Hawden from his feet. One look and then he could walk away for good.

'There is someone to see you, Mrs Charlton.'

Kat's attention was on the papers in front of her so that she didn't look up in response to Ellen's arrival in the room, only frowning her confusion when the house-keeper paused inside the door with her announcement. She hadn't heard the bell, or a knock at the door, so this hesitation, rather than going ahead and telling her just who had called, was puzzling. As was the strictly formal, 'Mrs Charlton'. The housekeeper usually just called her Kat.

Of course when Arthur had been alive, it had been dif-ferent. He had always insisted on the strict formality that he had been brought up with. But Arthur had been gone for almost a year now, and the regime he had imposed had been one of the first things that Kat had got rid of as soon as she possibly could.

'Who is it, Ellen?'

'He said to say someone from London,' Ellen said and her tone alerted Kat to the fact that this was not just any 'someone'.

But then she remembered just who was supposed to be arriving here today, and everything fell into place. Nothing had been the same around here for months now. Not since Arthur's untimely death and the awful discoveries that had been made in the aftermath of that event. And today was the day when she found out just where she stood. If she stood at all and wasn't lying flat on her face.

'Show them in, Ellen.'

She knew her tension showed in her voice. This was Arthur's solicitor after all, the person who held the details of their futures in her hands. And Ellen's future was tied up with the place every bit as much as Kat's own, as was the future of so many of the workers on the estate. So many more people who had been let down by her husband. That was one of the reasons why today was so important.

Her attention had drifted back to the papers on the table in front of her as she heard Ellen's footsteps cross the hall. If it was the solicitor then she really hoped there was going to be some good news. Something she could hope to work with. Some way out of all the worry and the uncertainty that she had lived with over the past few months. So many people depended on her, and she would really love to be able to help them.

The extent of the problems Arthur had left her with had made her mind spin. The gambling and other sordid ways he had spent his money had been bad enough, but the full details of appalling business debts that had followed one after another, like a row of dominoes falling, the foreign names, this one huge corporation—the Itabira Corporation in South America—involved in the financial dealings, had left her reeling. But one thing was clear. Her late husband had ruined the estate, spending every last penny they possessed on the secret life he had been hiding from her ever since they had married—even before then, she admitted. The truth was that she had never known Arthur Charlton at all.

The man she had married—the man she had thought she was marrying—had never existed. If she had even suspected half of what she now knew about him she would never have considered his proposal.

If their visitor was the solicitor, then she had had a sex change, she realised, as the footsteps that came back across the hall were much heavier and more forceful than Ellen's had been. Definitely male. And definitely some male who put his feet down, as her grandmother had used to say, like ready money. Hard and firm and strongly in control.

Behind her the footsteps had come to a halt. The sudden silence told her that her visitor was close, standing in the doorway. But before she could look up a voice spoke and the sound of it sent her world into a violent, dizzying spin.

'Hello, Kat.'

That voice...

Her mind failed her, refusing to complete the sentence. The words wouldn't form inside her head. There was no way it could be him.

'Heath?'

The word whispered from her mouth, the papers falling from her hands and onto the table as she forced herself to look up, to look towards the doorway. The man she saw there had an impact on her senses that made her whole world, her sense of reality, rock dangerously on its axis.

Hello, Kat. When she had thought that she would never, ever hear that voice again, it was almost as if he had come back from the dead and had walked into the room in some disturbing ghostly form. Back to haunt her present as he had her past.

'Heath!'

It *was* Heath. The same and yet not the same at all. This was a bigger man, leaner, more muscled, stronger, darker. So different and yet so much the same. The wild boy he had been, the youth with lightning in his eyes, danger in his fists, and trouble in his heart, was still there. She could see him still in those molten ebony eyes. But the untamed, unkempt boy was now hidden, concealed under a more forceful, powerful, more polished veneer. A gorgeously sophisticated, polished veneer. A forcefully male, stunningly sexy appearance.

This man stood tall and sleek, once wild jet-dark hair tamed into an elegant crop. The long, whipcord-lean body was sheathed in a superbly tailored steel-grey suit that hugged the contours of his powerful frame, clung to a narrow waist and long muscular legs that were now planted firmly on the soft surface of the cream and blue carpet, handmade leather boots gleaming black against the pastel colours. An immaculate white shirt heightened the darkness of his complexion, the tan that could only have been acquired from a long time—from *life*—in a country that had a much warmer climate than the Yorkshire moors. Around his shoulders hung a tailored black raincoat, unbuttoned and long, that made her think of some long-ago highwayman come to the door, pistols in his hand, ready to demand a ransom or that she hand over her jewellery. And—was that an earring that sparkled against the olive skin of one ear lobe? A brilliant, deep green emerald that winked in what little light there was from the window. An ornament as fantastic and unexpected—and as exotically beautiful—as the man who stood before her.

'It really is you.'

Once she would have been so happy to see him. But that had been in the days when they had been such friends. That was someone who was long gone, probably for ever. After the way they had parted, the dark threats he had tossed over his shoulder as he left, she knew that friendship was no longer what he felt for her or any member of her family. If his stiff and hostile body language, the cold glitter of those deep dark eyes, the unsmiling expression said anything it was that he had not come here for a nostalgic reunion.

And because of how it had once been between them, that look left her feeling shockingly and shivering cold.

From a distance she heard his voice again. A man's voice, deep and husky and touched by that unexpected and totally foreign accent. A voice she knew and yet had never heard before.

'Who else were you expecting?' he said.

The total lack of warmth in his tone sliced into her like a blade of ice, making the ground suddenly unsteady beneath her feet, her legs as unsupportive as cotton wool.

This man who had been such a vital, and essential, part of her life. So much more than a friend who had shared her childhood with her, the loss of her father, the beginnings of her adolescence, stood with her against her brother's tyranny, and had then just vanished. Walking out without a word of explanation, and making no effort at contact ever since. She'd cried her loss into her pillow for more nights than she cared to remember but he had put her right out of his mind, it seemed. She had not seen or heard from him in almost ten years.

Now, 'Hello, Kat,' he'd said. And that was all it took to turn her world upside down.

But then that was what he had threatened to do. He had said that one day he would be back and then he would turn the life they knew on its head.

'Who else did you think it might be, Miss Katherine?'

The touch of cynical humour, the dark mockery was new. Like his appearance it was so far from everything she had ever known of him. Her Heath had never looked like this. The Heath she had known had never had that sleek, sophisticated grooming that made him look like some glossy honed predator, who had prowled on silent paws, dangerous and alien, into the very civilised atmosphere of the home she had built. But then, she of all people knew how 'civilised' appearances could be misleading.

But in spite of that sophistication, that grooming, he still looked like some creature of the wild that was barely under control, eyes watchful, every muscle poised and taut ready for fight or flight—whichever was necessary.

No, looking into his eyes she saw no hint of flight at all. The old Heath was there in the burn of defiance in those golden eyes. A rebelliousness that no sophisticated clothing, however he had come by that, could ever conceal. When she looked up into his face it was to see a man who had the features of her long-ago friend and yet none of the warmth that had ever shone between them. Heath was here, but the boy she had known was gone and she missed him. The pain of it was like a stab to her heart.

'Miss Katherine!' she managed, breathless and uneven. Mocking the stiffness of his tone in the same moment that her heart lurched in discomfort at the sound of it. 'You always used to call me Kat!'

'You were Kat then.'

It was shockingly cold and distant and his eyes might have been shards of black-coffee ice in his tanned face. He slid the long coat from his shoulders, tossed it over the back of a nearby chair, and the sudden transformation from bold highwayman to sleek gentleman was such a shock that it actually had her breath catching in her throat.

'But it was a long time ago,' she told him stiffly. 'We were nothing but children. Didn't know any better.'

And in all that time had he learned nothing? Heath could only ask himself. He should have known better than to come here like this. He had told himself that he had come back for one reason only, vowed that he would deal only with the two men who had made his early years such misery. The men who had treated him like an animal and not a human being. He would come back to Hawden to show them what he had become, to reveal the power he now had over them, throw their insults, their cruelty, in their faces, and walk away, never once glancing back.

That plan was well in hand, at least as far as Joseph Nicholls was concerned. Arthur Charlton was a different matter. When he had learned of the other man's death he had felt like a hunter thwarted of his prey. Denied the satisfaction of facing down the earl, he had burned with frustration. And that frustration had driven him where he had sworn that he would never go again.

Back into the presence of Katherine Charlton, who had once been Katherine Nicholls. The woman who had taken what little was left of his heart when life, her brother and his best friend had finished with it, and stamped on it, crushing it cruelly under her slender foot.

'We are no longer children.' He nodded. 'And we haven't been for a long time.'

And that was where the mistake he had made had been born. With memories of the few happy years of his childhood surfacing once he was back in England, he hadn't been able to resist coming to the Grange just once. Hadn't been able to fight against the need to come here and see just what Kat had become, what the years had made of her.

Just one look, he had told himself. One look at the woman she was now and then he would walk away.

But that one look had been fatal to his peace of mind. Fatal to his determination to walk away from Hawden and all it had once meant to him, shaking the dust of the place from his feet. That one look had told him that he couldn't walk away from Katherine Charlton. One look was all that it had taken to show him that he still wanted her, still hungered for her more than he had ever wanted any women in his life. He had to put her away from him, move back from her both mentally and physically before the hunger that burned along every nerve destroyed his ability to think with the cold logic that he knew this situation demanded.

He had known that she would still be attractive. How could she have ever been anything else? Even as a girl she had always drawn all eyes.

He hadn't known that she would turn into such a beauty.

Time had taken her long-limbed form and made it softer, more womanly, with the sort of curves that made his pulse rate kick into heated action. In the years since he had last seen her, her wild coltish, tomboy looks had been smoothed down, refined into this elegant ladylike creature who looked like a pale reflection of the Kat he had once known. Her long dark hair that had once hung untamed around her face, tumbling onto her shoulders, was now smoothed back into a sleek ponytail that swung when she moved her head. Her face had thinned, creating slashing cheekbones under the deep blue eyes, and those eyes looked huge, wider than ever, framed by lush thick black lashes. Even dressed in a simple blue cotton dress she looked every inch the lady of the manor, totally at home in the house where they had once peered in through the windows from the outside, fascinated by being forbidden to enter.

'Oh, we're definitely not children any more!' Kat laughed, though it was a laugh with no humour in it. 'We've left all that well behind us.'

He could practically feel the chill from her words, the bite of her response and her eyes had darkened in angry rejection of him.

The curt, sharp words might be flung into his face, meant to distance her from him as clearly as the way that she stepped back, away, but they did nothing to quell the heated sting of attraction that spiralled through him. Senses burning in instinctive response, he surveyed her from the indignant, defiant face her chin brought up so that she was looking down her aristocratic nose at him, to where her feet, in delicate blue sandals, were placed firmly on the thickly carpeted floor.

'You are certainly no child. Every inch the lady.'

The flare of something in her eyes told him that she recognised the way his tone had deliberately been pitched so that the words were not a compliment. She must know so well what had been behind them.

Because the exclusion from the Grange had been just for him, he remembered on a twist of savage bitterness. Kat had never been barred from what the locals called 'The Big House'. The night that the guard dogs had heard them in the garden, racing to attack the intruders, and grabbing Kat by the leg, powerful teeth ripping her skin, she had been taken into the house and made welcome, her hurts tended to, a bed provided for the night. He had been ejected forcibly, tossed out into the lashing rain like a stray, unwanted, flea-ridden cur. And when he had returned to High Farm, Joseph had taken a riding crop to him for daring to have the nerve to trespass on their aristocratic neighbour's land.

That was the last time that he and Kat had ever been truly close. That experience had taught her what luxury money could bring, the pleasures of being cared for in the soft comfort of the Grange. When she had come home she had seemed like a different person, more like her brother's sister rather than the untamed tomboy she had once been. She had moved further away from him with each day that had passed, and now here she was, still reserved, still distant, with her cool blue eyes showing that she too regarded him as an intruder into her elegant world.

Well, he was more than an intruder. And one day soon she would learn just how completely their positions had been reversed. Once he would have rushed to tell her. The man he had become knew how to wait, knowing it was worth it in the end.

'I've grown up,' she threw at him now. It was like ice, cold and sharp as her gaze. 'I should hope that we both have.'

Oh she'd grown up all right. Grown up and further away from him than ever. The childhood friends they had once been no longer existed. If in fact they had ever truly been as close as he imagined. Looked at her coldly, he could well imagine that she had just been whiling away her time with him while the fancy took her.

But thinking coldly was almost impossible. He had once wanted this woman with the hunger and need of a lonely boy's heart. But she had turned away from him, choosing instead to give herself to a man with the money and the position she craved. He was no longer that lonely boy who had fought himself for her as well as the rest of the world. And the feelings she stirred in him were nothing to do with youth but the hard, demanding hunger of a mature man. A man hardened by life and experience.

A man who wanted the woman before him with a hunger that had been growing inside him for ten long years, even when he had tried to deny that it existed.

Even when he had told himself that he would just take one look at her and walk away. He had actually believed that he could do just that. But that had been before he had seen the woman she had become. A woman who in the space of a few moments had woken a hunger in him that he knew would never subside easily or stay under control for very long.

He had come for revenge on her brother, on her husband who had escaped him by dying unexpectedly. But the truth was that he still had unfinished business with

Lady Charlton. Unfinished business that he had refused to let himself recall how deep it went until now.

'A lot of water has passed under the bridge since we were last together,' he said, ironing every trace of what he had been thinking from his tone. 'Things are no longer the same.'

'They're most definitely not.'

Mental discomfort pushed the words from Kat's mouth. She didn't know quite how to behave in front of this man who was and was not Heath. Certainly not the Heath she had known.

The ice in his eyes told its own story. And there was something in that 'didn't know any better' that turned her blood cold in her veins. She was not dealing with the Heath she had known, or anyone like him. The new lines on his face, etched around his mouth and eyes, lines that could not by any stretch of the imagination be described as laughter lines, told their own story.

'How could anything be the same after so long?' she demanded, hardening her tone to match his expression. 'You don't deserve a welcome after ten years' absence and silence. To be silent all that time, you can never have thought of me.'

'A little more than you have thought of me, Miss Katherine.'

Brutal cynicism made a dark mockery of the once respectful way that her brother had insisted that Heath should address her. This Heath, this man who had so obviously made a success of his life, would never now submit to calling her Miss Katherine or the deference that her brother had once so insisted on. This man clearly stood tall and proud, looking the world right in the eye. And the way he used that polite title lashed at her, seeming to scour

off a layer of skin, leaving her feeling raw and exposed
underneath.

'Or perhaps I should call you Lady Charlton, now.'

'It is my name!'

Nervousness made her toss it at him in a way that even
she acknowledged sounded cold and distant. It was a tone
worthy of Arthur Charlton himself, and as such it made
her wish she'd never spoken. But then it only matched
Heath's own approach tone for tone. If he had not come
back as a friend, then he could only be an enemy, and she
suddenly felt the need to be very wary of this almost complete stranger. He had prospered, that much was evident.
But prospered in what way, in what field?

'You know about my marriage, then?'

And she could just imagine how he would interpret
it. But he had no idea how her life had been since he had
left. No idea of the hole he had left in her existence and
the ways she had tried so desperately to fill it.

Heath nodded slowly, his dark face set and cold as if
carved from the rock on the moor outside; his eyes just
shards of flint, opaque and unrevealing.

'I heard of it and decided that one day I would call to
offer you my congratulations. I didn't think that your husband would have left you a widow before I could do so,
and that those congratulations would instead mean that I
had to offer my condolences.'

'Arthur's death was a shock to us all.'

What else could she say? It was just the truth after all.
And the words were the polite fiction she had been hiding behind ever since the day the police had arrived at the
Grange with the shocking news. But the real truth was
that she had been hiding the reality of her marriage for
far longer than that. So much so that the instinct to conceal, not to let anyone see what had been hidden behind

the respectable, elegant doors of 'The Big House' had become second nature to her now. Her instinctive, fall-back position. The one that protected her from things that were so much worse.

That was what marriage to Arthur had reduced her to. The marriage that the whole of the neighbourhood—the county—had considered the wedding of the decade but had soon proved to be such a bitter lie from start to finish. The marriage she had been hoping to try to move on from when the discovery of just how Arthur had left things had knocked her right back.

'And it has rather changed things.'

'It has? How?'

But Heath offered no answer to that question, instead he moved into the room, prowling across the carpet in a way that revived her thoughts of the predatory wild cat of moments before. Standing before the huge windows, he affected an absorbed interest in the scene before him, the wide expanse of the garden, the swimming pool tucked away at the side of the house, and beyond that the range of fields where sheep grazed contentedly in spite of the rain.

Where he stood in the light from the window she could see the marked skin of his cheek, the thin scar that spoiled it, running along one cheekbone. And the memory of how he had come by that, who had put it there, caught at her nerves and tugged them hard. The mark that had been made by the glancing blow of a cast-off horseshoe, flung with deliberate viciousness at him by her brother Joseph in one of his irrational rages. The horse Joe owned and had ridden at a local show-jumping championship had been well and truly beaten by Heath's own mount, loaned to him by her father. Typically, Joseph had taken out his fury and his jealousy in an act of violence that had horrified her.

Had Heath been to see her brother as well as coming here? Just the thought of the confrontation between them made a sensation like cold footprints slide down her spine, making her shiver in uncomfortable response.

That 'decided that one day I would call to offer you my congratulations' scraped painfully against her already too-taut nerves. It implied that he had been planning his return for some time. If he had come back earlier would anything have been any different?

A bitter memory sliced into her mind. That of arriving at the village church on her wedding day not quite four years before, and standing at the back of the aisle, just inside the doors. The organ had already begun the familiar notes of the 'Wedding March' but just for those seconds she had paused, looked around. Looking for one dark, harsh but infinitely familiar face. Allowing herself just a moment's—what?

Hope?

But of course Heath hadn't been there. Her brother and Arthur had treated him appallingly. There was no way he would want to be there to witness the joining of their two families in marriage. He had been the only one to warn her against the Charlton family. If she had listened to him then she might have spared herself so much heartache.

'How has that changed things?' she repeated, her tone insisting on an answer.

'Isn't it obvious?'

His turn was slow, almost dance-like, pivoting on his heel as he came face to face with her again.

'You own all of this.'

A gesture of one strong hand took in the whole of the house, the garden and the estate beyond the window.

'Little Miss Kat has got everything she wanted. The big house, the status, the oh-so-elegant way of life...'

He wielded his words like a rapier, flashing, stabbing, making her wince inwardly. Everything he said revived the memories of the last time she had seen him, the anger that had flared in him then. And later his total rejection of her. The bitter burn of the knowledge of how far she had been from having 'everything she wanted' made her lash out in self-defence.

'Not *everything* I wanted!'

If only he knew that she had never had any sort of a marriage, not in the real sense of the word. That the man who had been such charming, witty and attentive company through her teenage years, helping to distract her from the empty space in her life where Heath himself had once been, had turned into a petty and increasingly malicious tyrant almost from the moment that he had put a wedding ring on her finger on her twenty-first birthday. That the big house had become a hated prison; the elegant way of life nothing but a lie.

'My husband died!'

'I know… But that's no great loss. Though originally it was your husband that I thought I would have come to see.'

'Why? What did you want with Arthur?'

'We had—business to discuss.'

The emphasis on that word 'business' sent a shiver of warning down her spine. So many 'business' meetings lately had resulted in worse news piling on bad news.

'What sort of business?'

'It's hardly relevant now.'

Heath's expression deliberately blanked off so that she could have no idea what was going on behind those opaque ebony eyes.

'I can't believe that Arthur would ever want to do any business deals with you. He never said anything about it.'

'Your husband talked about his business with you?'

Was there something else behind that question? Something that put the darker note into his voice?

'Well—no.'

Arthur hadn't talked to her about anything if the truth was told. He had issued orders, insisted on how things were to appear. But she had only been a couple of weeks into her marriage when she had discovered that a trophy wife was all her husband wanted. A woman who could look elegant at his side, display around her neck or dangling from her ears the jewellery that was the Charlton heirlooms everyone knew about, and organise the society parties he put so much emphasis on.

Of course she now knew just why those parties were so important to him. The image they had been planned to present to the world while he hid the reality behind a smokescreen. The truth had been that he had never really wanted a *wife*, not in the true sense of the word. Their marriage had been as fake as the 'heirlooms' that were really only paste copies, the originals sold long ago.

'That—wasn't Arthur's way.'

'I thought not.'

His response caught on her nerves. It took her back to his declaration that he had business to discuss with her late husband. What connection had he had with Arthur's business dealings?

The question had formed on her lips only to be caught back sharply as the sound of light, hurrying footsteps in the hall gave notice of a new arrival. And knowing who it must be, Kat knew she couldn't continue her questioning now.

CHAPTER TWO

THE door swung open and the slim, blonde-haired figure of her sister-in-law came into the room. Isobel had obviously been into town on a shopping spree. Half a dozen elegant carrier bags swung from her hands and she had the smug look of someone who had just given her credit cards a hammering.

Inwardly Kat sighed at the thought that she and Isobel were going to have to have a heart to heart about their situation. Obviously the younger woman had not taken in—or had refused to accept—the gravity of their situation. Quite frankly she was amazed that those credit cards hadn't bounced. They very soon would. Once all their creditors realised the seriousness of the situation there would be a huge number of final demands for payment.

But that was a showdown she didn't want to have in front of Heath. Isobel was so like Arthur in her determination to go her own way and listen to no one. So she forced herself to keep calm, even to smile at Isobel while inside every nerve was screaming a protest at her sister-in-law's actions.

'I've had a fantastic time!' Isobel declared. 'Lacey's had their new summer range in and they had some gorgeous stuff. I...'

Her voice trailed off as she caught sight of the tall, dark

man standing by the window, a silent, watchful observer of this new arrival in the room.

'Hello!' she said, the rising lift in her voice, the sparkle of her smile making Kat's heart twist, her nerves tugging painfully as she recognised the signs she knew only too well.

Isobel had spotted someone she fancied. That much was obvious. And the man who had sparked her interest was none other than Heath. Which Kat supposed shouldn't have surprised her. Compared with the skinny, scruffily dressed boys her sister-in-law usually hung around with, Heath was all man. His height and his bearing seemed to fill the room, those deep-set black eyes burned like burnished jet under dark, arched brows and when he smiled...

Dear heaven, when he smiled, his face was transformed, Kat admitted, feeling her stomach twist and lurch almost as if she were on board a ship that had suddenly pitched sharply downwards in the waves. It was shocking to realise that this was the very first time that his sexy mouth had even curved into any sort of a smile or that his forcefully carved face had shown any warmth, since he had appeared in the room so unexpectedly.

'Hello, Isobel.'

It seemed as if that trace of the accent on Heath's words had deepened, darkened, making him sound so much more exotic, so much more foreign.

'You know who I am?' her sister-in-law was definitely intrigued and the smile that played over her mouth was a blend of curiosity and provocation.

'Of course. You are young Isobel all grown up.'

'And you are?'

Isobel fluttered her long, mascaraed eyelashes flirtatiously, and Kat felt the twist of something cruel in her

heart as she saw Heath switch on another swift, easy smile
in response.

It was even more shocking to realise that the sharp burn
of reaction had a double-edged source, one that made her
mouth dry in horror as she recognised it for what it was.
When he smiled, Heath looked so very different, so devastatingly sexy that the heat of her response was like a
flash of electricity along her nerves. But it was blended
with something else, something that was far less comfortable to endure. Deep in her memory where she had tried
long ago to bury it, she could hear the echo of Arthur's
voice, vicious and savage-toned. *You're still dreaming of
your bit of rough—that gipsy. That's what turns you on.*

'Don't you recognise Heath?' she put in hastily, rather
too sharply.

'Heath?' her sister-in-law queried. 'Heath who?' And
the jolt of realisation brought Kat up sharp against the
fact that she had no idea how to answer that question. She
hadn't even thought about what Heath might be calling
himself now.

She hadn't thought of *anything* beyond the fact that he
was here, back in her life again.

'Heath Montanha,' Heath supplied, those dark eyes of
his still fixed on Isobel.

And no wonder. The girl who had been little more than
a child at eleven when Heath had left the village all those
years before had blossomed in the time he had been away.
She was a small blonde bombshell, curvy and sensually
glamorous, beside whom Kat always felt too tall and rangy,
taken back to the tomboyish adolescent she had been who
had never quite fitted in anywhere.

Anywhere but with Heath.

Remembered pain twisted in her gut as she recalled
how once he had always been at her side, her friend, her

support. Heath had never needed to belong in the way that she had longed to. He had laughed at the girls who had thought they were so cool, turned his back on any need to be conventional or fashionable. It had been her own need to find the femininity that she had felt had been so lacking in herself that had drawn her to the sort of society offered by the Charltons. That had ultimately led to the 'dream wedding' that was supposed to give her everything she had ever fantasised about.

A dream wedding that had opened the door to a private nightmare.

'Heath Montanha?'

Not Nicholls, Kat added to herself. Well, who could blame him? Obviously the thing he had most wanted to do once he was away and free of the village was to discard the name of the family he had never belonged to in the first place. And the name of the man who had once made his life such hell.

'Such an exotic name! What nationality is that?'

Isobel was openly flirting now, her voice light and teasing, her smile straight into those dark, watchful eyes.

'It's Brazilian.'

'You went to Brazil? Why there?'

It was Kat who asked, unable to suppress her curiosity.

'Why not? After all you were the one who once told me that my father could have been an emperor of China.'

Memory stabbed like the sharpest stiletto as she recalled the light-hearted way they had created an imaginary ancestry for him. A rich, powerful background that would enable him to hold his own against Joseph and Arthur's tyranny. They had been on the same side then. And she had believed that nothing could come between them.

'You remember that?'

'I remember,' Heath acknowledged and the emphasis he put on the words sent a shiver down her spine.

What else did he remember? And more importantly, *how* did he remember it?

'I'd love to go to Brazil.'

Isobel was determined to drag Heath's attention back to her. Not that there was any dragging needed, Kat acknowledged. Isobel had always had the effect of an open honeypot on men. Men who had never looked at Kat in quite that way. Certainly men of the type that Heath had become had never looked at her like that.

Even her husband had never looked at her in that way. Not even on her wedding day, when every woman had the right to feel beautiful. As soon as they had been alone, he had criticised her appearance and set himself to try to change everything about her. It was only later that she had come to realise just why he had been that way.

'Rio de Janeiro...the sun—the sea—samba dancing.'

Isobel let her curvaceous body sway in time to imaginary music inside her head.

'But don't you think you should offer our visitor some refreshment, Kat? How long has he been here and you haven't even offered him a drink?'

'I was just about to.'

It wasn't the truth and a quick sidelong glance from Heath's dark eyes told her that he knew that only too well. The thought of her sister-in-law reproving her for her neglect of hospitality for the man who as a boy had always had the door of this house slammed in his face twisted something deep inside. She had no doubt that exactly that thought had come to him too.

She had once promised herself that if she had ever found herself in a position of wealth and comfort where she could welcome Heath then she would do so with open arms. Now she was exactly where she dreamed of being but too much had come between them to ever let that happen.

'Perhaps I should ring for tea. If you would like that ...'

The words were barely out of her mouth before she was hearing in her own head how they must have sounded to Heath. And seeing the way that his lips curled she could almost read just what was going through his mind. That she had deliberately played the 'lady of the manor' card, offering afternoon tea as if she were her mother-in-law and not a young woman of nearly twenty-five. Though the truth was that she hadn't felt young for too long. Not for almost four years.

'Tea?' he drawled mockingly. 'How very English.'

'Well I am—we are English,' Kat snapped defensively, her tone too sharp for politeness as the suddenly vicious twist to his beautiful mouth said only too clearly.

'While I am just a mongrel, hmm?'

There was open challenge in those blazing jet eyes now. Challenge and a dark, cynical derision that had all the tiny hairs on the back of her neck stiffening in wary sensitivity.

'That isn't at all what I meant!'

'And why not? It is true after all. I am of mixed blood as you always suspected—and not pure-bred English like you and your family.'

Memory stabbed again at the thought of how they had once speculated on just what his ancestry might be, what exotic background could have created his dark dramatic looks.

'You found out about your true background?'

'I did. And your husband would have been delighted to know that it was every bit as far from his aristocratic pedigree as he always believed it was.'

And he wasn't going to enlighten her any further, his

tone declared adamantly. He had no intention of letting her in on anything he had found out about himself. If anything marked how wide the chasm that divided them had become then it was that.

'Are we having this tea or not?'

Isobel's impatiently petulant voice broke in on the intense concentration of his gaze on her face, making those deep dark eyes blink just once, slowly, before he deliberately looked away, in the direction of her sister-in-law.

'Perhaps not,' he drawled silkily. 'You'll forgive me if I don't stay. I have business to attend to.'

He was picking up his coat as he spoke, tossing it over his shoulders like a cloak as he had worn it on his arrival, and turning towards the door. That was the second time today he had mentioned business deals but never explained himself. Once more that icy sensation slid down her spine.

I'll be back one day. And then you'll see how everything you think you have can all be turned on its head.

Suddenly afraid that he would walk out of her life again as he had done once before and that this time he would never come back, she hurried after him.

'Heath—wait…'

He was almost all the way down the long, tiled hall, never hesitating or looking back. But then, just at the last moment, he paused and turned back very slowly.

'You never said why you came. What you are doing here.'

'Why did I come to the Grange today? Surely the answer to that is obvious.'

'Not to me.' Her voice croaked embarrassingly as she forced out a response.

Heath smiled briefly once again. It was a smile of ice, totally without any hint of warmth in it.

'I came to see you, of course. Why else would I be here?'

'To…'

'To see you, Lady Katherine,' Heath repeated, the words sliding over her like a stream of ice water, making her skin shiver miserably. 'To look into your face just once and then walk away—this time for good.'

CHAPTER THREE

THAT had been the plan, Heath acknowledged.

He had told himself that he would just see what she had become, and then walk away. He would shake the dust of the Grange from his feet and go back to the life he now had—a life of success and power, so very different and so very distant from the life he had once lived—endured—here in Yorkshire. If her husband had still been alive then he might have stayed, to have the satisfaction of seeing his plans all fall into place, his revenge become complete. He would have enjoyed seeing Arthur Charlton and Joe Nicholls brought as low as they had once brought him. Nicholls already knew why he was here, knew that he had lost everything, and until now Heath had thought that that would have to be enough.

But that had been before he had come face to face with the woman that Katherine had become. Seeing her, seeing the stunning woman she was now, feeling his heartbeat quicken, his blood pulse through his veins, his body hardening in yearning hunger, he had known that he could no more turn and walk away than he could cut out his own heart and throw it at her feet as she had once made him feel he might.

He had thought that he was over her, but seeing her had taught him, in the space between one heartbeat and another, that that thought had been desperately deluded. There was no way he was 'over' this woman. It had nothing to do with revenge, and everything to do with passion, with the sexual hunger that ate him up from inside—and always had—just from knowing that Katherine Nicholls existed.

If he had wanted her once when she was a girl, before she had developed into the full power of her beauty, then now he felt that he would die if he didn't have her in his bed, just once. If he didn't know the full satisfaction of making love to her, feeling her soft body underneath him, opening to him, hearing her cries of delight as she reached her climax.

And she would come to orgasm; he had no doubt about that. No woman could look at him in the way she had done in the first moment that he had walked into the room without a blistering connection between them on the most basic, most primitive level. The burn of awareness that had been in his body had been reflected in her eyes. He had seen it looking back at him from their once-cool blue depths, turning them molten and cloudy, the pupils so wide they seemed to have darkened the whole of her eyes.

And he had known then that he couldn't stick to his original plan and walk away. He wanted her too much to do so. More importantly he wanted her *to want him* as much as he had ever hungered for her. And most of all he needed her to acknowledge it. Publicly. Only then would it heal the scars of the slashing wounds she had once dealt him.

Fancy Heath? You have to be joking! she had said to Arthur Charlton and the scathing note on her tongue still burned like acid in his memory. *I mean—look at him? No money, no job—no class! The Nicholls family may have*

*fallen on hard times, but we do have some pride. How
could anyone want him?*

He had come here for revenge but his vendetta had been
against her brother and her husband and that was being
worked through just as he planned. The financial dealings
that had yet to be revealed might have given him a darker
satisfaction, one of the mind, but this was personal. This
would bring a very different sort of fulfilment. A heated,
sensual, carnal satisfaction. One that already had his body
tightening and hardening in anticipation of the delights to
come.

'You did that once before,' she said now, her voice unexpectedly rough at the edges. 'The walking away bit.
When you left I thought that was for good.'

'So I did—and if I had had my way, had any sense, I
would have stayed away.'

He'd meant to stay away. Meant to sever all connec-
tions with Hawden and the life he had had here but fate
had intervened. The dirty tricks and bad deals Charlton
and Nicholls had tried to pull on one of his companies,
not knowing who owned it, had revived so many bitter
memories. Once and for all he had resolved to deal with
the two men who had made his early life such a hell. But
he had taken some time to put his plans into place, make
them watertight. And in that time Arthur Charlton had
fallen victim to his decadent, sordid lifestyle so that now
there was only Nicholls left to deal with.

But he hadn't reckoned on the fact that Kat would still
have this devastating hold over him. That he would take
one look and find himself incapable of walking away.

'But other matters brought me to Hawden...'

'What other matters?'

Heath smiled down into her face.

'I have scores to settle, as you must know.'

Looking into her defiant, long-lashed eyes, Heath suddenly knew a twist of the double-edged sword that his plan for revenge now offered him. All he had to do was to tell her why he was here. Reveal all the cards he held in his hand—and he did hold all of them; he had made damn sure of that before he had even left Brazil. Everything was signed, sealed, tied up so watertight that there was no chance of even a single item in this house, on this estate sliding out of his grasp. He had the Charltons and the Nicholls exactly where he wanted them and all he had to do was call in their debts…

But where was the satisfaction in using that against Kat? What sort of gratification could he get from taking a sledgehammer to this situation when he could do things so much more subtly? Much more enjoyably. No, he didn't want her to know yet why he was really here.

Joe and Arthur had robbed him of money and position. Kat's betrayal, her rejection of him, had been something different. A betrayal of the heart, of the soul. He would show her how it felt to have your heart taken and stamped on.

He would make her want him as much as he wanted her. After all, if she fell for him now it was only because he was wealthy, because of who he had become. She had never wanted the Heath he had been.

But he didn't want to blackmail her into his bed. He needed her to come to him willing—wanted her to come to him wanting, needing, *hungry*. Because she couldn't help herself. As he couldn't help himself where she was concerned.

She already did; he could see it in her eyes. But she was damned if she'd admit it. She would admit it before he was done. She'd admit it and come to him and beg him to take her. He had never forced a woman in his life and he didn't intend to start now.

The youth he had once been would have thrown any caution to the winds and reached for her, grabbed her... But he was no longer that adolescent. Time and experience had taught him the wisdom of holding his counsel, hiding his true feelings. Once he had told this woman how he felt and she had laughed in his face. There was no way he would ever risk that again. This way he would get what he wanted and more.

'S—scores to settle.' She took a step back from him, mentally at least even if she didn't move at all physically. 'Against who?'

She already knew the answer, Kat acknowledged privately. If he had come back to 'settle scores' then he could only have come looking for the men who had treated him so appallingly in the past. But how far did his need for vengeance go? Who else would be included in it?

Once again that cold cruel smile flickered over his lips, bringing no light to eyes that remained as cold as polished jet.

'You have to ask? Your brother—your husband too, were he alive.'

'And me?'

'I told you—I wanted to see you just once.'

It was so softly spoken it sounded almost gentle. But there was nothing gentle about the burn of those dark eyes, the way that his beautiful mouth was tightly compressed, taking all the sensuality from it and turning it into a cold, hard line.

'So now you've seen me—what?' She didn't know what she was asking for. What she wanted the answer to be.

This time that smile was positively feral. It stripped away all the apparently civilised control he had imposed from the moment he'd walked into the room and replaced it with a cold, fierce anger. Under the veneer of sophistication and worldliness he was still the wild, untamed creature she had once known. The dangerous, wild-spirited creature who had answered to no one.

'I told you—I'm leaving. You'll have to forgive me if I decline your offer of tea.'

Could his voice have been any more mock-polite, the slap in the face effect any more deliberate?

'You're not coming back?' The thought of losing him all over again tore at her heart.

'That depends...'

'On what?'

'On you.'

'What do I have to do with it?'

His impatient twist of his head, the brilliant emerald in his ear lobe catching the light and sending sparks flying, told her how irritated he was with the question.

'I would have thought that that was obvious. Do you want me back—will you welcome me here?'

How she wished she could answer that straight. How she wished he could still be the Heath she had once known, the Heath she had longed to have back again. But that was not the Heath who now stood before her. And she was no longer the Kat she had been as a child.

'I thought not.'

She had hesitated too long. And those cold black eyes had seen the doubt in her face, the way she had had to rethink her decision.

But what else could she say? She had looked into that dark closed face and known a new and very different feeling from one she had ever known before. One she had never experienced with Heath in all the time she had known him. She looked into his hard-boned face, into the deep black pools of his eyes, saw the jet-hard gleam that was in them and knew...

Fear.

Fear was what she sensed, what she felt crawling over her skin like ice-cold footprints marking out a path along every nerve. A sense of dread that warned her that something was to come, something that brought danger and darkness into her life along with this man who had once been her friend.

Who was so obviously her friend no longer.

'I will leave you to your tea.'

Heath was turning away again, obviously taking her response for dismissal and, for all the turmoil of emotions tangling inside her, Kat couldn't let him go like this. Not with everything so raw between them. With so much she wished she could say if only she could find the words.

'Don't...'

She wanted to reach out and stop him, but at the same time the shivery warnings held her back so she didn't know whether to move forward or not. Her legs seemed to tangle together, her feet tripping over each other as her body fought with her mind.

Suddenly several things happened at once and she didn't quite register any of them until it was too late.

Her steps faltered, feet catching on a raw edge of one of the tiles, pitching her forward in the same moment that Heath paused, turned back. She was falling, heading for the floor and unable to do anything about it, her breath leaving her body in a shaken cry, when Heath's instincts kicked in, swift and sharp. His arms came out to catch her, whipcord muscles taking her weight and holding tight, hauling her up before she hit the ground.

The movement swung her round, still off balance, so that she landed hard against the strong wall of his chest, her breasts crushed against his ribs, her head just over the heavy, rhythmic thud of his heart. The scent of his body, warm, clean skin mixed with some cologne that had a tang like lime, surrounded her, making her head swim. Only his strength held her upright, her eyes blurring in sudden confusion—and something else that shuddered through her like a heated pulse.

For the space of a couple of raw, uneven breaths, she felt him tense, distance himself as far as he could without actually moving away from her, knew that her own body had stiffened too, in shock and unease. She knew that she should pull away but couldn't find the strength to do so. And in the same moment she felt a terrible sense of danger, blending with an equally stunning sense of having come home. The two sensations warred with each other, pulling her heart, her mind in different directions so that she didn't know which one to act on. Indecision held her still, frozen, unable to think, scarcely able to breathe.

But then his grip on her arms loosened, hands smoothing down to where the skin was exposed by the short sleeves of her dress, the warmth of his palm stroking over her skin in a way that took that sense of shock and disorientation with it. The tension eased, changed, seeped away, and her heart skipped a beat, the sudden release letting her relax against him.

'Kat...'

She heard his voice above her head, the warmth of his breath stirring her hair and she allowed herself a smile; her sense of relief a glow that lit her up from inside. Perhaps she had been reading everything so wrong. But she had barely recognised the sudden gentleness, given herself up to it, when a heartbeat later all that tension and more was back but in a new and very different way.

'Katherine...'

From a distance she heard his voice again. A man's voice, deep and husky and touched by that unexpected and totally foreign accent. A voice she knew and yet had never heard before.

Was this truly Heath? Was this her childhood friend; the companion of those wild, carefree days? This man looked like him. But Heath with the lighting of wildness burned out of him, the deep polished jet eyes cool and assessing, not flashing with fierce defiance as they had done in the past.

'Heath...'

It was as if she was trying his name on for size. As if she had never spoken it before or the person she used it for were a stranger, a newcomer into her life. A man who filled her senses, surrounded her so that she inhaled him with each breath.

Somehow she managed to tilt her face up towards his, and this close there was no avoiding the changes in him. She could see the faint lines that time had etched round his nose and mouth, feel the scrape of the late afternoon's growth of beard at his hard jawline, see the tiny flecks of grey at the temples of that black-as-night hair. From this angle the scar that Joe had inflicted on him was a distinct dent in his skin, a harsh white mark against the tan that he had brought back with him from wherever he had been.

But that was when her thought processes stopped. When something changed. She couldn't have put a name to it, couldn't have explained it in any way. She only knew that it was as if the air she breathed had become charged, filled with sensual electricity so that it burned its way down to her lungs, searing the ends of nerves on the way.

'I...' she tried but the electrical storm had melted her brain and no more words would follow the single syllable.

'You?'

She saw that beautiful, sexy mouth twist, almost smile. But the next moment Heath's grip tightened, cruel fingers digging into her arms. She was hauled up hard against him and fierce lips came down brutally on hers.

For a moment everything was wild heated delirium, running burning and demanding along her veins. The world spun round her, any sense of reality lost in its stinging haze. She was burning, melting, losing herself. Out of her mind and out of her body.

He had never kissed her before. She had never felt his lips on hers, only on her cheek, and once, awkwardly, on her hair. Their friendship had never been like that. They had held hands, hugged—hard—but never kissed. Not as a man kissed a woman. But she had never been kissed this way before. And she had never known that it could make her feel like *this*.

This was something she had never experienced. This flare of heat and power, this rush...

Of hunger?

Sexual hunger?

Was that the aching, burning sensation uncoiling in the pit of her stomach, spreading like wildfire along her nerves? A heady pulse seemed to have started between her legs, making her stir restlessly, her body as agitated as her mind that whirled in confusion and disorientation.

Was this what it really felt like? What a woman was supposed to feel for a man? Was this what had been missing in her marriage all along? Had Arthur been right? That she had never been a real woman—until now.

The thought shocked her, even frightened her, her heart thudding in a very different way. Her mind seemed to split in two, warring between wanting to sink into this, into his arms, into his kiss, take more of it, take all of it—and the almost panicked need to pull away, tear herself out of his grasp and put as much distance between herself and this shocking blaze of heat as she possibly could.

'Heath…'

She muttered his name against his lips, meaning it as a protest but finding that it only added to the dangerously erotic sensations his mouth was creating. The taste of his skin against hers was a smoky, sensual tang, the movement of her lips opening to him so that his tongue slid along the seam of her mouth, then dipped in, tasted, teased. Tormented.

It was too much. Too intimate. Not what she wanted and yet so much what she craved. She tried to pull away, tried to twist from his arms, but he simply shifted his position, held her closer. One long powerful hand scored into her hair, grabbing at dark brown strands of it and twisting sharply, angling her head so that he had her exactly where he wanted her.

This time his kiss was very different. If that first kiss had been the kiss of a conqueror, a kiss of dominance, of power, then this was surprisingly, shockingly gentle. A kiss of enticement, seduction, of temptation. Slow and sensuous, provocative, arousing, it seemed to steal her soul out of her body, melt the bones in her legs so that his strength was the only thing keeping her upright. She softened against him, swayed. Too close. So close that she could feel the heat and strength of his body under the fine clothes.

Fine clothes that Heath had never worn, never owned before. Fine clothes that spoke of another man. A man so very different from her childhood friend that just the thought of him set up a fearful trembling in her limbs, tightening each nerve, stretching it almost to breaking point. She didn't know this man. And yet he was so familiar.

His body seemed to call to hers, waking it and stirring it in a way no one else had ever done.

And hers to him. Because she was now so close that she could feel the hard, swollen evidence of his physical hunger for her pressed tight against the cradle of her pelvis.

'Kat!'

From inside the sitting room, Isobel's impatient voice floated out to them.

'What *are* you doing?'

Shock froze Kat's thoughts, startled her into total stillness, her mouth still captive under Heath's, her mind lost in the sensual haze that had taken possession of it. She felt his sudden check too, the jolt that brought him back to the present, the stiffening of the powerful frame that just a heartbeat before had been pressed so tight against hers that it was as if they were blended into each other, not two spirits, but one.

For the space of a couple of whirling seconds the world seemed to hang suspended, out of focus, all sense of reality lost. But then Isobel spoke again, her tone more petulant and discontented.

'Kat, I really need that tea.'

As if from a distance she heard Heath's sudden, sharp bark of laughter, harshly cynical, drawn from some deep shadowy place inside him. And the mood that had held her captive and lost shattered once and for all. Heath lifted his dark head, took a step back. He distanced her from him too, setting her back on the floor so that only now did she become aware of the way that she had actually been lifted right off her feet, her toes barely keeping contact with the decorative tiles underneath her.

With a sudden snatching breath reality came back to her and she was dropped back into the world. But a world that no longer seemed the same. A world that now seemed turned upside down and inside out and she was suddenly sure would never be the same again.

What was happening to her? Who was the woman who had just gone up in flames in Heath's arms? Surely that couldn't truly be her?

Without thought her hands went to her hair, trying to smooth tumbled strands that he had twisted and tangled up so mercilessly. The band that had held her ponytail was lost, pulled free and abandoned somewhere on the floor. So she had to content herself with the rough and ready combing out of the knots that those powerful fingers had created. Her dress too was crumpled, caught up high on her thighs when he had lifted her and now she tugged nervously at the material, trying to restore it to some sort of decency. And all the time she didn't dare to lift her eyes to look at Heath; to meet the burning ebony gaze that she knew by fearful instinct was fixed firmly on her face.

He waited, silent and dark, an ominous shadow on the outer edges of her vision while she struggled with her appearance, making no comment, taking no action. Just waiting and watching. Until at last she could find nothing else to force her attention onto, nothing to keep her from looking in his direction. And she had, unwillingly, to lift her eyes to his.

Immediately she felt as if she had lost herself in the darkness of his gaze. His focus was intense, his lids half lowered, hiding the full force of his stare behind the fringe of lush, thick lashes. A faint smile played over the sensual mouth, his lips still stained by the rush of blood that the pressure of their kiss had created. But that smile had nothing of warmth in it, nothing of concern. It was a dark sense of triumph that curled the corners of his lips. The smile of a predator who had the tastiest sample of prey right in front of him, just within perfect pouncing distance.

And in the back of her mind, echoing cold and cruel, Kat heard again the words he had tossed at her only a short time before.

I have scores to settle, as you must know.

They had sounded dangerously ominous then. And they sounded so very much worse now. How could she have let this happen—with Heath? The Heath who had come back to settle scores, and had stated it openly. So had that kiss been part of that aim for revenge? He couldn't fake his arousal but what had been behind his actions in the first place?

She felt as if a cruel hand were squeezing her heart, twisting it inside her. How was it possible that at long last she had reached out and touched something of what it really meant to be a woman—but with this man? A man whom she couldn't trust with that stunning, newly tasted sensuality any more than she could ever have trusted her husband?

'If you knew how long I have wanted to do that.'

Heath's voice was low, husky, and so unexpected in the long drawn-out silence that had descended between them that it made her start, her head going back nervously.

'I've waited for years…'

'And you'll wait every bit as long before you ever do it again,' Kat tossed at him, her mental unease, the lingering tremors of the emotional whirlwind that had swept through her, making her voice colder and harsher than she had planned.

If she had thought that her sense of reality had been rocked before, now she felt she was losing her grip. How could Heath even say that? He couldn't have been harbouring such thoughts about her back then… Could he?

The thought of her former friend, her protector, looking at her in that way, thinking about her that way, combined with the trembling reaction of her own feelings to rock her world on its axis.

Heath's tone was darkly cynical and a black eyebrow lifted, questioning her assertion.

'Is that a fact, Lady Katherine?'

Triumph. Predator. Prey. Scores to settle. Every one of the words that had been inside her head when she had pulled back from his kiss just moments before slammed again at the sound of the taunting question.

'Are you trying to claim that that was not what you wanted? That you were not totally involved—totally enjoying... My apologies....'

Kat blinked at the abrupt change of subject at the end of his speech, the even more startling change of approach and intonation. Even his face changed, that contemptuous, sneering look vanishing and his expression becoming warmer, softer—he actually switched on a smile.

Was he really *apologising* to her? It seemed so impossible but then as her vision cleared she realised that Heath was no longer looking at her, but those polished-jet eyes were focused on a point over her shoulder and behind her.

Isobel of course.

'I apologise for keeping you waiting,' he murmured smoothly now. 'But Lady Katherine and I had—some catching up to do.'

How could one face express so many emotions at once, especially when none of them was true? His mouth was smiling, but close up like this she could see the almost brutal control that made it curve, fighting against the tension in the muscles in his cheek and jaw that revealed the way he was not in a smiling mood at all. His head was turned towards her sister-in-law but there was something about its position, an angle, an inclination to one side, that told her his attention was really on her, waiting and watching from the corner of his eyes to see her reaction. And those ebony eyes had a cold and cruel glint in them that warned that every action, every expression, was carefully calculated for the effect he wanted.

Heath had never used to keep his feelings so carefully masked. He had had a wide, wicked grin that had surfaced when he was happy—not that that had been so visible in the last months they had been together. If he was angry it blazed in those deep black eyes and clamped his mouth into a tightly compressed line. The hatred he felt for her brother and Arthur had been like a hard, brittle mask he had worn, the only tiny movement in an icily set expression being the way that his mouth curled into something approaching a snarl that was positively feral in its fury. He had worn his heart on his sleeve or at least on his face.

But now his expression seemed as smooth and slippery as polished ice. Apparently expressing one thing while somehow managing to reveal that the truth was the exact opposite. And the watchful tension in the long powerful body so close to hers communicated yet another emotion. One she was actually frightened to try to interpret because it reflected so closely the stinging burn in her own skin. The way that every nerve, every cell seemed to be vibrating with newly awoken yearning. The hunger that his kiss and his touch, brief as it had been, had sparked off inside her so that she felt as if electrical pins and needles were travelling along every vein.

And the thought that he might feel the same made her shiver, but whether with horror or delight she had no way of knowing.

'I'll leave you to your tea...'

How had he managed to make such an innocuous line

sound so sardonic and potentially dangerous? And how could he switch from the hot, dark passion he had shown just moments before to this easy smoothness without his voice or his expression letting him down? She was still feeling ragged around the edges as if parts of her skin were unravelling and leaving her nerves rawly exposed.

'If you're sure you can't stay.' The carefully polite words came automatically after so many years of trying to do what Arthur had wanted, what he had insisted on.

'I'm expected elsewhere.'

'Are you staying in Hawden?'

Her voice didn't sound like her own inside her head. Deeper than before, slightly husky, was this the voice of the Kat she had never yet been able to see?

He shook his dark head.

'No.' Those black eyes slid to her face, calculating and cold. 'I'm at High Farm. Your brother invited me when I called round there...'

'No! You can't be!' Kat couldn't hold it back. 'Joe would never...'

'You think not?' Heath questioned on a note of mockery. 'I assure you that Joseph insisted I could not stay anywhere else.'

'Then I don't envy you,' Isobel put in, giving a delicate shudder at the thought. 'High Farm has gone to rack and ruin since Kat moved out. There's no one there to look after things. You'd be much more comfortable—'

'I'm sure that Heath will manage,' Kat put in suddenly, fearful that her sister-in-law was about to suggest that she should offer him a spare room to sleep in.

'I am sure that I will,' he agreed with deliberate irony. 'After all I have known much worse.'

That glinting black gaze challenged her to comment on that but she knew she didn't dare. Of course Heath had

known so much worse. In the past he had barely been allowed inside the house never mind to sleep in a bedroom.
There had been a small lean-to at the back of the house,
draughty and without any electricity. He had been ban-
ished there after her father's funeral and had never slept
inside again. Guilt twisted inside her at the memory of
how, at fifteen, she hadn't been able to persuade Joe to
change his mind over that. She had always wondered just
why Heath had put up with it. Why he had never fought
back but had put up with her brother's worst excesses with
a grim fortitude for so long. It was only later that he had
turned his back on them.

'But believe me, your brother has given me a very different welcome this time.'

He was turning as he spoke, had left the house and was
striding down the path without a backward glance before
she had absorbed that double-edged remark. Watching
his tall, powerful figure walking away, Kat found that her
thoughts were tumbling over each other, twisting, tangling,
none of them emerging clear and open for her.

'Your brother...' Isobel was saying, her voice carry-
ing disturbingly clearly out of the open door so that Kat
knew without hope of salvation that Heath must hear it
even halfway down the path. 'How did they know each
other?'

'Heath used to live at High Farm. He worked in the
stables.'

'The gipsy boy? He was *that* Heath?'

Kat could only nod silently. Because she was watching,
because she couldn't look anywhere else, she had caught
the single second of hesitation in Heath's walk that told
her so clearly that he had heard Isobel's comment, caught
the stunned intonation in her voice.

She winced inwardly, knowing how he must feel to hear

the old disparagement echoing down through the years. But this time the sense of sharp discomfort that slashed through her had its source in dread *of* Heath rather than fear *for* his distress as it always had in the past. Comments like that had been commonplace back then, but, seeing the man he had become, now only the most foolhardy, or those who didn't know the truth, like Isobel, would risk using them now.

Scores to settle.

Once more those words echoed ominously inside her head, making her shiver in apprehension. There were only two men whom he had hated enough to travel all this way—from another continent!—to deal out his revenge for past hurts after all this time.

Her brother and her husband.

But death had frustrated the reckoning he had hoped to make Arthur pay, so now, like a savage predator, thwarted of his prey, where would he turn for the satisfaction that he had come looking for?

Her hand crept up to her mouth, fingers pressing against her lips that still felt bruised and tender where Heath's savage kiss had crushed it only minutes before.

Just what had that kiss meant? It had roused those explosive, burning feelings in her that she only barely understood and certainly had had no experience of before, but Heath had remained icy cold and unmoved, not even touched by it, it seemed. Oh, he had been aroused physically, but any emotions that went with it had been ruthlessly suppressed, if in fact they had ever existed.

'So *that* Heath's back?' A thread of slightly nervous excitement ran through Isobel's voice as she watched Heath's retreating figure. 'Well, I never expected he would turn out this way.'

Neither had she, Kat admitted.

The day that she had once dreamed of, longed for, had finally arrived and it was nothing like the way she had once allowed herself to hope it would be. The boy she had wept for, had ached to see, was here in her life again but nothing was as she had ever dreamed it could happen. The boy she had cried over no longer existed and the man Heath had turned into was as dark-hearted and dangerous as any wolf that might once have prowled the moorland, hunting for prey to tear to pieces in its fangs.

And now he was heading for High Farm where he had said that her brother had invited him to stay.

Scores to settle.

Cold shivers of panic seared through her and had her rushing for her phone, speed-dialling the number. She could hear it ringing at the other end of the line.

'Come on, come on!'

Her toe tapped impatiently on the floor while her fingers drummed a tattoo on the table top. In her ear she heard the ringing going on and on...until suddenly the tone changed and the call was put through to voicemail.

'Oh, Joe!'

There was no way she could leave a message for him. She couldn't put into words the wild, unformed fears that were swirling inside her head like the storms that sometimes devastated the moors outside.

'I don't know why a man like Heath would want to stay at High Farm—why anyone would.'

Isobel had lost interest in having tea and was gathering up her shopping, preparing to head up to her room.

'The place is a dump. No one in their right mind would want to set foot inside there.'

Her sister-in-law couldn't know how her words woke memories inside Kat's head. Memories of the way that just that word had been used to describe High Farm when she had been growing up there. When she had felt that she never quite fitted in at the school she had been sent to, the other girls mocking her tomboyish character, her lack of style, the well-worn clothes she had dressed in. High Farm had been a 'dump' then, and under Joe's care—or, rather, lack of it—it had only grown worse.

But even living in a dump, she had been happier than she was now, or had ever been in her marriage, surrounded by the luxury and glamour of the Charltons' lifestyle. A glamour that, she had learned too late, concealed a dark heart that she had never even suspected when she had first come into the Grange and seen it and its inhabitants as so very different from her own feuding family. Life had seemed so much simpler then.

Heath had seemed simpler too.

She wanted that time back. She wanted her life back as it had been when she was young, before her father had died. When everything had been warm and clear and—yes, innocent. But you couldn't go back—they said you should never go back. There was no way she could recapture that wild innocence.

The boy Heath had been no longer existed, just as the girl she had once been had turned into the woman she now was. All those years in between had changed them for ever.

And thinking of the way she had felt in Heath's arms, the power of his kiss, the impact it had had on her—the way she still trembled in reaction; the stinging electricity like pins and needles was only now starting to ebb away—Kat had to ask herself if she really did want to go back to a time when they had been just friends. When there had been nothing like this in her life, to startle, excite and—yes—to frighten her as well.

Once more her hand crept to her mouth, seeming to feel

again the crushing kiss that Heath had pressed against it. Just remembering sent the burn of hunger searing through her again. She'd never known that hunger before. Never realised how it could really feel to be a woman.

She knew what had happened to her. As a woman she had reacted to the strong, powerful, sexy man that Heath had become. But what had Heath been feeling? What had he meant by that kiss? Had it just been the gesture of power and possession it had seemed or had the sexual hunger she had sensed in him meant something else?

Shaking her head, she switched off her phone, knowing that there was no way that Joe was going to answer now. She would have to go up to High Farm and find out just what was going on.

In the living room the grandfather clock started striking the hour, making her realise that it had barely been sixty minutes since Heath had walked into the Grange.

Sixty minutes and things had changed so totally that she had no idea at all just how she should go forward. With no way of knowing exactly what Heath might feel, what he might be planning, she couldn't even begin to guess what part he might play in her future.

CHAPTER FOUR

'THE place is a dump.'

Isobel's words were inside Kat's head as she made her way over the rutted, potholed road that led into the farm-yard at High Farm the next day. And there was no way she could deny them. The house she had grown up in had been neglected enough when she had been a child. Her mother had died when she was seven, and they had struggled to look after the big old farmhouse with the small and irreg-ular income that her father had managed to eke out. Later, Joe's young wife had come to live there when Kat's brother had taken over the land on their father's death. But Frances had been a delicate woman, her weakness aggravated by an early pregnancy when she had struggled with constant sickness. She had shown no interest in doing anything to improve her surroundings, and only survived until shortly after her son was born when an undetected weakness in her heart had killed her.

Poor Frances had hated High Farm, Kat reflected. She had married Joe, believing him to be a landowner of some status and had been brought to this neglected, rundown property so close to the wild moors. It was no wonder she had tried to cultivate the company of the Charltons and had sided with Joe when he had been determined to push Heath out of his home and into the ranks of the farmhands.

They would need his room as a nursery for the baby, she had said, and Heath had been sent to sleep in a lean-to at the side of the house, only coming in to the kitchen for his meals.

Just the sight of the farm, dark and foreboding, made her shiver and pull her jacket closer around her as protection against the wind. Built in the nineteenth century—there was the date 1875 etched into the stone above the heavily carved dark oak of the main door—and positioned at the top of a hill that gave it its name, it had once been the grandest building in the neighbourhood. Built of the local harsh grey stone, it had narrow windows, deeply set in the walls, protected by shutters. Inside, as she knew, those windows gave very little light, and the whole impression of the place was of a building armoured against all comers. The high chimney stacks, one over the kitchen and the other leading to the main sitting room, were redundant now but she had memories of how, when her father had been alive, the fire in the living room had been lit on Christmas Day, turning the rather spare, ill-furnished room into a haven of warmth and delight.

But without that fire the inadequate central heating made High Farm a cold and draught-ridden place. Even the trees at the end of the house were stunted and permanently bent by the wind. Why had Heath chosen to come and stay here when he could have been so much more comfortable in the village, or some hotel in the nearest town?

'Joe?'

The house was in darkness, no lights switched on against the gloom of the day, and the silence sent unease creeping over Kat's skin as she made her way to the living room. She had wanted to come here yesterday, the sense of apprehension and uncertainty that had nagged at her ever since Heath had left making for an uncomfortable, restless night. But no sooner had she put the phone down on the vain attempt to contact her brother than the solicitor from Leeds had arrived and the bad news she had brought had tied her to long, worrisome discussions so that she hadn't had the heart for the trip to the farm in the dark and the rain.

Joe hadn't answered his phone that morning either and she hadn't been able to settle to anything else until she came to find out what was happening.

'Joe?'

'Who is it?'

If the roughness in her brother's voice hadn't already given the game away, then the way that he suddenly lurched up from a chair, swaying uncertainly on his feet, confirmed everything she had anticipated and most feared. Joe had been drinking again. And drinking on top of a hangover from last night if the look of his heavy, bleary eyes and unshaven face was anything to go by.

'Oh, it's you...'

His welcome, or rather the lack of it, did nothing to ease her concern as she switched on the light, then regretted the action as seeing her brother more clearly only made things so much worse. Had he even gone to bed? His clothes looked as if they had been slept in.

'Joe—what has happened to you?'

'*He* happened to me!' her brother snarled, not bothering to explain who 'he' was—not that Kat needed any such explanation. Every fear that had been lurking at the back of her mind now came rushing back in full force.

'Who?'

'Who do you think?'

Swaying more dangerously, he reached out to grab hold of an arm of the chair to steady himself. But it was clear that he was not safe on his feet.

'Joe—sit down.'

With a hand on his arm she eased him back into his seat, wincing at the wave of stale, whisky-soaked breath that wafted over her as he did so. She had known that Joe had had a drink problem for some time, though he had refused to listen to any advice or warnings. But this was worse than anything she had ever seen before.

'I told you he'd come back, damn him. Heath Monta… whatever he's calling himself now.' He spat the name out as if it were poison

'Heath's been here?'

She knew that already; hadn't Heath told her himself that he was staying here? But it seemed that echoing Joe's replies and adding a question to them was the only way of getting the answers she needed.

'Yes, he's here. Of course he's here. Back again like the bloody bad penny—or, rather, the cuckoo in the nest.'

'Ah yes,' said a voice from behind her, smooth and silky but with a definite edge of steel that made her flinch inwardly. 'The cuckoo in the nest now as once before.'

Joe's eyes flickered towards the man who had come into the room, but didn't focus and he swore under his breath as Heath strolled towards them. But Kat turned to watch and having looked couldn't look away again as she struggled to adjust to yet another image of the new Heath.

Dressed in tee shirt and jeans, he should have looked so much more like the younger Heath, the boy she had once known who had no smart outfits, nothing but the sort of clothes that were suitable for work on the farm. He had rarely worn anything but denims and tee shirts—but never like this. The immaculate white cotton clung to the honed lines of his torso, outlining the defined muscles, the broad, straight shoulders down to the tight, narrow waist defined by a broad leather belt, and the worn denim shaped lean hips, long long legs. Somehow this faded denim managed to look both expensive and classy, nothing like the battered, grubby jeans that he had combined with a ripped and misshapen tee shirt in the past. And the Heath who had just come in from the fields or the stables had never worn a pair of such perfect-fitting, handmade soft leather boots.

In spite of the darkness of the day, the gloom outside the window, Heath still managed to look vibrant, vivid, alive. So very sexy with the glow of health on his tanned skin, the gloss of his rich dark hair, the gleam of the single emerald earring dark and vivid in the lobe of his ear.

'But perhaps you should remember how the cuckoo operates Senhor Nicholls,' he drawled now as he strolled into the room. 'He grows bigger and stronger until he can edge out the rest of the fledglings. One by one he pushes them over the edge, and out to meet their fate on the cold hard ground. And then—just like me—he owns all of the nest. Has it all to himself.'

'You—'

Shocked into staring in a way that she knew betrayed her nervousness, Kat got slowly, warily to her feet, easing up from her position half kneeling beside her brother to face the dark intruder into what had once been her family home.

'Are you claiming that you own High Farm?'

Heath's smile was brief, dark, dangerously cold.

'Not claiming, Lady Katherine—I am stating a fact.'

'No…'

Kat shook her head violently, sending her loose hair swinging out around her face. She knew that she must have lost colour, could practically feel the blood seeping away from her cheeks.

'How can you say—?'

'He does…'

It was Joe's voice that cut in on her, low and mumbled but enough to stop her dead and make her turn again to stare at him in appalled surprise.

'He does,' Joe repeated, his eyes sliding away from her shocked gaze and closing tight. 'He owns the whole damn place. Lock stock and barrel.'

'I told you I was staying here.'

It was Heath who supplied the comment, calm and smooth, as he pushed his hands deep into the pockets of his jeans and leaned back against the wall, his negligent posture totally at odds with the sharp, assessing scrutiny of his gleaming black eyes.

'Staying, yes,' Kat replied tartly. 'But you neglected to point out that you were here as the owner and not as my brother's guest.'

'Would you have believed me if I had?'

No, Kat was forced to admit. She wouldn't have believed him. And yet why not? The truth was that the thought of Heath Montanha owning the farm where he had once been little more than a servant, one of the hands who worked the land, was no more unlikely—in fact less so—than the idea of her brother actually inviting into his home the man with whom he shared a savage mutual hatred. Heath Nicholls as he had been once might have struggled even to lay claim to a single stone in the farmhouse building, a tiny speck of the fields surrounding it, but Heath Montanha as he had become was a very different prospect and, much as she might wish that she could, there was little hope in Kat's thoughts that she might be hearing wrong.

So, 'As of when?' she managed to force herself to ask, wincing inwardly as she fought to control the quaver in her voice.

'As of last month.'

Heath hadn't moved away from his indolent position against the wall, hadn't moved a single muscle in order to straighten up, but she sensed the change in his attitude as he spoke the words, the way that he was waiting and watching, ready for her response and knowing exactly how she would react. So she swallowed down the burn of bitter shock and fury that rose up into her throat and tried desperately to surprise him by turning what she hoped was a blank and unrevealing face towards him. One that hid the struggle she was having for composure.

'So long? And you didn't think to mention it when you were at the Grange yesterday?'

'Oh, I thought of it,' Heath assured her carelessly, tossing the words her way. 'But then I had second thoughts about it too. I knew that you would find out the truth soon enough—and that it was better coming from your brother…'

'Better!' Kat's mood broke away from her control, the words escaping on a snap of anger in spite of everything she tried to hold them back. 'Better, how? How would it be better to learn that you have taken over my family home… Just how did you come to own it?' she questioned abruptly, distracted from her anger at his words by the sudden disturbing thought.

Joseph had never mentioned the deal. Surely he would have said something if the transaction had been any sort of legal, honourable process. Fear and anxiety were zigzagging their way along her nerves.

'In a card game.'

It was flat, cold and the icy glance that accompanied it seemed to stab right to her heart. She had to reach out for the back of the chair to steady herself and could only shake her head in disbelief.

'No—never...'

But beside her, Joe was shaking his head, muttering something thick and unintelligible into his chest as his head slumped to one side. Heath barely spared him a flicker of a glance as he fixed Kat with his polished-jet stare.

'What? You don't think that your brother would be degenerate enough to enter a casino? Or you think he's too good a card player...?'

'I didn't think he'd be fool enough to pledge the house—the farm...'

The horror of the truth suddenly slapped her right in the face so that her head went back, her knees threatening to buckle under her.

'Damn bad hand...' Joe cursed. 'Just needed one good card...'

'*All* of the farm?' Kat managed.

'All of the farm,' Heath confirmed with dark satisfaction. 'Lock, stock—not that there is much stock worth considering—and barrel. And even that doesn't pay off his debts. He still owes me.'

'Still? Joe?'

But her brother had other things on his mind.

'I don't feel good...' he moaned. 'I'm going to be...'

Heath had moved before he could finish the sentence and before she had fully registered just what Joe meant. Her brother was hauled from his chair, carried bodily from the room into the kitchen, the door slamming shut on the ugly scene that resulted.

By the time Kat had hurried after them, her brother was half on and half off the worktop, a damp cloth being roughly applied to his face and stained shirt.

'I'll put him to bed,' she said jerkily, then realised what

she had said. 'Always assuming that he does still have a bed here?'

'Same bed, same room—for now.' Heath nodded. 'I'll get him up there for you.'

It was only as she followed him as he bundled her brother up the stairs that Kat realised how long it had been since she *had* visited High Farm. She had never actually been upstairs when she had visited and now she was forced to face the truth of just how the place had been left to go to pieces. The bedroom and the bed that Heath eventually dumped Joe's unresisting form onto were dingy and musty, the room smelling as if it hadn't been cleaned for weeks, the sheets grubby from overuse. At the windows, the curtains were half on and half off the rails and Joe moaned as what little light there was hit his half-open eyes.

Surprisingly, Heath crossed the room and tugged them closed, before he surveyed the attempt Kat was making to pull the covers up over her brother, his mouth twisting as he heard the other man's mumbled protests.

'He'll need to sleep that off—and he'll feel like hell when he wakes up.'

Not that he cared, it seemed, Kat told herself as he turned on his heel and headed out the door without a backward glance.

She was still trying to get Joe's shoes off when, totally unexpectedly, Heath came back in. He had with him a glass and large bottle of water that he placed on the bedside table, easing the bottle top slightly open as he did so.

'If he can get any of this down him then he'll pull round a bit quicker.'

'Thank you.'

Her voice was gruff, awkward at the unexpected consideration he was showing, but she hoped that Heath would take it only as the fact that she was struggling with the tangled knot in the laces of her brother's shoes. The burn at the back of her eyes threatened tears and made the task even more difficult than ever.

'Here...'

The touch of a cool, calm hand stopped her, startling her and making her jump back in shock. She regretted her response as soon as she saw his face, saw the way that his beautiful mouth tightened, a muscle clenching then releasing in his jaw.

'Let me...'

Unable to find any response, she simply waved her hand in the direction of the unyielding knot and stepped further back.

'There...'

Heath had released the knotted laces. Pulling the shoe off, he tossed it to the floor where it fell with a dull thud that seemed unnaturally loud in the sudden silence.

'Thank you—' Kat began again, but Heath shrugged off her response with an abrupt flick of his head, hunching one shoulder as if in rejection.

'I did think of bringing some painkillers in with the water, but the state he's in that wouldn't be the wisest move. Who knows how many he might take, and I really have no wish at all to end up with a dead body on my hands.'

'I would have thought that that was what you'd really want—hating him as you do.'

The shock of seeing Joe in such a state, the build-up of stress that stretched her nerves too tight pushed the words from her lips without a thought for whether they were wise—or even accurate.

'All your problems would be over then...'

She only knew how wrong she had been, the terrible

mistake she had made when she saw the flare of fury, the bitterness of cold rejection in the depths of his eyes.

'I'm so—' she began but Heath had already turned from her, marching across the room and out of the door with a fierce speed that told without words the sheer force of his anger.

Her conscience delivering a sharp, swift slap, Kat was forced to hurry after him, almost running to catch up. Even then she was still at the top of the stairs when Heath, taking two steps at a time, reached the bottom and looked to be heading out of the house. In the yard, beyond the windows, she could see his big, sleek, powerful car and knew that if he got into that before she could get any closer then he could drive away at speed before she had any hope of speaking to him.

'Heath—please!'

She didn't even know if he had heard her; didn't really expect any sort of response. But unexpectedly he came to a halt in the hallway, so abruptly that she ran straight into his broad, straight back, knocking all the breath from her body. The heated electricity that had seared its way through her yesterday burned along her nerves once again as she felt the heat of his skin through the fine cotton of his tee shirt, inhaled the clean scent of him.

Her own skin seemed to shiver in response to the sensations that were sizzling through her. Her legs felt as if they were weakening, the bones melting in the sudden rush of heat that was like lava flooding her veins. Her breath was harsh and tight in her lungs, catching both on the way in and out so that she gasped in raw and nervous shock as she struggled for control.

'Please...' she said again and didn't know even in her own mind just what she was asking him for.

Out of the corner of her eye she saw his dark head go

back, then he stiffened, moving carefully away from her and pivoting on his heel to turn to face her. The glitter of his eyes threatened to burn until she felt she might shrivel where she stood, but at the same time her whole body felt suddenly cold and shockingly lost without the hard warmth of his against it. But there would be no living with her conscience if she let fear put a rein on her tongue now.

'I am truly sorry.'

He was going to have to let her think that he had accepted that apology, Heath acknowledged to himself. There was no other way that he could hold onto his self-control and keep himself at this side of the room, with any sort of much-needed distance between them.

It was either that or reach out and grab her, haul her up against him and crush his mouth to hers as he had done once before.

And vowed never to do again.

Even if his blood thundered in his veins, pulsing so hard at his temples that he couldn't hear himself think. Even if his whole body hurt with the aching hunger that had hardened and tightened every inch of him in the space of a single, heavy heartbeat. Even if the scent of her body, the mixture of some aromatic perfume, the tangy lemon of shampoo on her hair and the clean fragrance of her skin was drying his mouth so that he could barely swallow. He could hardly breathe either, and the red mist of desire that threatened to swamp his eyes blinded him to everything else around him except her face. Her eyes fixed on him, wide and deep sea blue, shocked but so *aware*; drawing him in, dragging him under.

And those pink rose lips, slightly parted, that he longed to capture and take as his. Force them open with the pressure of his kiss, slide his tongue along the line where they parted, slip it into the warm moistness of her mouth.

Hell, no! No. He was not going down that path, even if every inch of him that was male responded to the call of her femininity in the most basic, primitive manner. He could indulge that need; he knew it without thought, without a word being said. It was there in every glance she turned on him, every breath she took. He had felt it when he had kissed her—the first kiss—just once, after more than ten long years of hunger and yearning. He could have her now. Kiss her into submission, take her up against the dark, dirty wall of this neglected hallway and he would swear that she wouldn't even fight him.

And he would have gone that way once. In his youth he wouldn't have thought twice about it. Young and wild, and as horny as a tomcat, he had operated only on instinct, on hunger, on need. He had never held back from taking what was on offer from the women who found him attractive—and there were plenty of them. But Katherine Nicholls had been a very different matter.

Lady Katherine Charlton was a very different matter. The woman who looked at him as if his touch would stain her skin, his kiss taint her mouth. The woman whose blue eyes turned to blazing sapphires as she fought with the need she didn't want to feel. The hunger that *he* made her feel.

He had sensed that hunger in her kiss. In the tiny whimper she had made under his mouth, the way her body had melted against him. And he hadn't even touched her. But one day he would. One day she would leave all her pride in the dust and she would come to him. One day she would beg for his touch. If there was one thing that the long years since he had last been in Hawden had taught him, it was that he no longer had to snatch at things, to demand them with the fierce rage of youth. He had learned how to plan, to analyse, to set up a situation where there was no chance of any outcome but precisely the one he wanted. Then all he had to do was to wait coolly and calmly for what he wanted to come to him. And the waiting, the anticipation, only made the fulfilment all the more delicious, more satisfying.

He could wait. And enjoy that anticipation.

'No matter what your brother may think I am not an irredeemable brute,' he tossed at her now, his voice cold from the struggle not to show anything else.

'I know.'

She actually looked shamefaced, colour rushing into her cheeks. Her sharp white teeth dug into her lower lip until he ached to reach out and stop her, stroke his thumb along the soft pink flesh that she was injuring, kiss away the small indentations that made his guts twist deep inside just to see them marking her mouth.

'I should never have said that. I didn't mean it.'

'I might have thought just the same way, once.'

Heath knew his reply stunned her. It was there in the way that her head went back, the beautiful blue eyes clouding in shock. She was fighting for control of her mouth, her expression and the knowledge of that gave him a kick of dark satisfaction low down in his body.

She was definitely off balance and that was just how he wanted her. It was as she turned her head so that the light caught the faint sheen of something that might have been tears glistening in those stunning eyes that something caught on a raw edge of his conscience, twisting uncomfortably, reminding him that this was not the way he wanted to bring her to him.

'Hell knows, I've wished him dead often enough,' he admitted roughly. 'But I've learned a lot since then and one of the things I know now is that it is true what they say about revenge being a dish best eaten cold. There is a lot more satisfaction in savouring the taste.'

His words seemed to slither nastily down Kat's spine, making her shiver inwardly. Once more she felt the tearing pain of loss for the Heath who had once been her friend—or had he? Remembering the way he had changed towards her in the last months before he had left, the cold determination with which he had turned his back and walked out of her life, she was forced to wonder whether he had simply been biding his time until he could get away from the whole family. Had he really ever cared for her or had he just used her as someone to fill the empty spaces in his cold heart before he had left to build this new and very different life?

'They also say that revenge is a poison meant for others that we end up swallowing ourselves.'

'I'll take the risk.'

Stark and bleak, it stabbed straight to her heart, making bitter tears burn at the back of her eyes once again, but this time for the loss of the person she had once thought he was. The boy-man she had loved so much it had hurt.

'In fact, I'll take the poison too—just as long as I take them down with me.'

How could anyone appear so bitter yet sound somehow lost all at the same time? She wanted to reach out to him, to take his hand and squeeze it hard as she had once been able to do when they were so much younger. But Heath's cold mask of a face seemed impregnable, armoured against any weakening emotion.

'Oh, Heath…'

The sense of loss choked her, knotting in her throat so that she could barely breathe. But if Heath heard the catch in her voice, the way it threatened to break on his name, then he blatantly ignored it.

'Go back to your brother, Katherine.' He tossed the command at her, an autocratic gesture with one hand indicating the way back up the stairs, away from him. 'You are needed there.'

Which was not the case right here. He didn't actually say the words but he didn't have to. Everything about him, his closed expression, the carefully blanked off eyes and tight jaw, his very stance, stiff and ruthlessly controlled, said it for him.

Needed by Joe. Not needed by Heath. Not even wanted as company. Dismissed.

She was turning to head back up the stairs when a thought struck her. Something—or rather someone—she should have remembered so much sooner. Guilt ripped through her adding another dangerous element to the already potentially explosive mix that was boiling inside her. She didn't want to turn back, didn't want to see Heath again, standing there so tall and dark and dangerous, silhouetted against the sky beyond the open door.

She certainly didn't want to feel the shivers of sensation that feathered her skin simply to look at him or know the moistening, melting feeling that took possession of her when they touched. But this was too important to let anything distract her from it.

'Where's Harry?'

The thought of her eleven-year-old nephew seeing his father in the state she had found him in tore at her heart. She knew how Harry felt, with no mother and only a father who neglected himself almost as badly as he neglected the farm to care for him. She hadn't seen him around so where was he hiding or...?

'At school where he should be.'

'But how did he get there? He can't travel all that way on his own. He—'

'I took him.'

Heath's reply was totally matter of fact but it still had the power to take her breath away.

'You... *You* took him to school?'

'And why the hell not?' Heath demanded. 'The kid needed to get to school and there was no one here fit to take him. It was only a ten-minute journey in the car...'

And an unexpected act of generosity from a man who had no cause to give a damn what happened to the boy, and every justification for hating him like his father. It had been Harry's expected birth all those years ago that had reinforced Joe's insistence that Heath had no place in the house.

'That was kind of you. Thank you.'

'Harry is just a kid. He has no part in this.'

'Yes—but...'

'Go back to your brother, Katherine,' Heath instructed again. 'That is where you are needed.'

And to emphasise his words, making sure there was no room for debate, he turned his back on her and walked out of the door. A few moments later she heard the roar of his car engine as he pulled away from the house, the spurt of gravel under the wheels heading down the drive. She had been dismissed. He had put her out of his mind completely.

And the shocking thing was how much it hurt. It stung bitterly, caught on every raw nerve in her head and twisted hard and tight.

Joe's sighing moan from upstairs brought her attention back to the present and the fact that, drunken idiot though he might be, her brother did need her right now. And maybe, just maybe, when he had sobered up—and recovered from the monstrous hangover that would inevitably follow his indulgence last night—she might be able to talk to him and they could work out what he could possibly do next.

Joe was fast asleep, snoring heavily as he lay on his back against the dishevelled sheets; she was not needed for the moment. Looking round the messy, grubby room, Kat shivered in shocked reaction. How had she never known that Joe had come this far down, that he had let everything slide? A row of whisky bottles were lined up along the top of a chest of drawers, further evidence of how bad his problem was.

And if he had come this low, then Harry…

For a moment, Kat covered her face with her hands, unable to bear the images that came into her mind.

Oh, dear heaven, how was Harry coping with his father in this state? She hadn't seen her young nephew for a couple of weeks, her mind so distracted by the appalling fallout from Arthur's unexpected death, so she had no way of knowing just how the boy was coping with his father sinking into this mire of neglect. She could only pray that Joe had had the sense to keep his drinking to the nights, when his son was in bed.

The brutal irony of the situation was the way that Joe had once been convinced that her marriage to Arthur would be the salvation of both families. Arthur would get the heir to the estate he needed to ensure it stayed in the family, and Joe's personal fortunes would be improved by the link with the aristocracy. That, she knew, had been behind his enthusiastic encouragement of her relationship with the Charltons. But nothing had gone the way he had hoped.

And the terrible thing was that she couldn't even offer to help. The news Arthur's solicitor had brought yesterday was that things were far worse than she had ever imagined. She didn't own the Grange any more, her late husband's debts were so huge that selling it, or, rather, handing over the estate to the huge corporation that already had a very large stake in the property was the only option. At least that way some of the workers on the estate would keep their jobs.

It was as the silence of the house descended round her that she suddenly felt a new sensation, a new realisation creeping over her. As if on a loop inside her head, Heath's words kept replaying over and over again.

'Go back to your brother, Katherine... That is where you are needed.'

Did he know how those words had stung, the pain of rejection and isolation they had made her feel? Of course he did, and that was why he had used them, deliberately dismissing her as unimportant and unwanted. The misery of loss iced her veins, turning to shock that zigzagged along her nerves at a sudden realisation.

Was this how Heath had felt when her brother had thrown him out of the house, sending him to sleep in the rough bed in the tiny shed? Back in the familiar surroundings of High Farm, she could recall that day so clearly that it was almost as if it were happening all over again.

They had barely accepted the news that her father was dead, taken by a sudden, shocking and unexpected heart attack, before Joe was back from university and throwing his weight around as master of the house. And he had reserved the special venom of his hatred for Heath. He had barely stepped through the door, hadn't even taken off his coat, when he had made his feelings plain.

'My father might have allowed you to stay in this house,' he had declared, cold and harsh as the winds that howled around the farm that winter night. 'And he forced me to tolerate your vile presence whether I wanted to or not. But my father is no longer here, and I'm in charge, gipsy boy.'

He flung open the door, careless of the icy drop in temperature as the vicious cold outside swept into the house.

'From now on, you earn your keep as one of the farmhands. And as one of the hands you no longer have any right to live, eat or sleep in this house.'

'Joe...you can't!' Kat had protested. She had to say something. She couldn't just stand by and let this happen.

Her brother ignored her, gesturing towards the door.

'Get out, gipsy. Get out—and stay out.'

'Joe...' Kat had tried again but the ferocious glare her brother had turned on her had made her mouth close unwillingly over the protest she wanted so desperately to make.

She knew her brother. She understood only too well just how being crossed, thwarted in any way, only made him so much worse, so much more intent on indulging the vicious side of his nature. To say more was probably only to condemn Heath to an even more hateful situation. But it felt so wrong... She just couldn't...

Kat shivered as she recalled how she had felt in those moments. She had been appalled, outraged, terrified all at the same time. But whether terrified for Heath or of what he might do she had no idea and the conflict threatened to tear her thoughts apart.

But then, just as in spite of everything she pushed herself to try again, she caught the look that Heath had turned on her. The cold anger, the ferocity of rejection in his glare, had her backing down at once. She might risk fighting her brother, but tackling Heath himself was a different matter. If he didn't want her protection, then she knew better than to offer it. If his fierce pride meant that this was his battle and he would fight it his way, she could at least let

him have that. Even if it was not what her heart cried out
to give.

The silence seemed so tight and brittle that she was
afraid that any word would shatter it. Her stomach tied
itself into tight, nervous knots, her heart thudding painfully, as she watched Heath tense, his tall body, still holding some of the rangy leanness of youth but starting to
harden into the full strength of a man, stiffening as he
drew himself up, chin angling defiantly. She flinched inside, waiting for the inevitable explosion, feeling stunned
and shocked when it didn't come.

Instead, Heath simply stared her brother down, keeping his deep-set black eyes fixed on the other man's pale
blue stare until Joe was the one who looked away, his gaze
dropping to the carpet, which he studied with obviously
assumed interest. Only then did Heath turn and walk away,
defiance and hostility in every inch of his long, straight
spine, the set of his powerful shoulders, his dark head
held arrogantly high as he strode out into the icy night,
Joe slamming the door tight shut behind him.

And now, knowing just a little of that terrible sense of
rejection that had assailed her before, the ache of loss and
loneliness at the realisation that she no longer really had
a home, that someone else had moved in and taken everything she held dear, Kat thought that finally—at long,
long last—she really understood something of the way that
Heath must have felt in that moment. When her brother
had thrown him out of the only home he had ever known.

It seemed that Heath had achieved the ultimate in revenge, by completely turning the tables on Joe and his
family. He now owned High Farm, he was sole master here
as Joe had once been so long ago. And just as her brother
had tossed him out into the cold and dark, she could have
little doubt that that was what Heath had in mind too.

CHAPTER FIVE

KAT would have left by now, Heath told himself as he brought the car to a smooth halt beside the front door to High Farm a few hours later. Joseph must be out of danger, sleeping off his drinking binge in his tip of a bedroom. She would have given up and gone home again, back to the civilisation of the Grange where she could still play Lady of the Manor for a little while yet.

For as long as he allowed it. He had instructed his representatives and his legal team never to let drop that his was the name behind the takeover of the Grange and all the other property Arthur Charlton had squandered to feed his gambling and drugs habit. The fortune he had handed over in extortion and blackmail payments so that his secret life would never be found out. Lady Katherine must know about that too by now, and as a result she would be only too desperate to keep the potential scandals quiet.

She would just be grateful that someone was there to take the ruinous debt off her back, even if it meant taking the Grange with it. That he was that someone was a detail he wanted to keep to himself for as long as possible. Only when he had what he wanted most from the wife of Earl Charlton would he let her know the full truth about the man he had become.

First she had to come to the man she thought he was.

And she would come because she couldn't help herself. She would come to the man who might own High Farm, but only because he had won it in a card game. The other Heath she would come to know in time. When it suited him.

The smell of something cooking—something warm and savoury and appetising—was what hit him first as he came through the door into the dark, echoing hall. Food? It was the first time since he had set foot in the house that there had been anything warm or welcoming—or even comfortable in the place. He had been shocked to see just how much Nicholls had let it go to seed in the time since he had taken over from his father. So much for his wild boasting that now he was master here and everyone would know that the new generation had taken over from the old.

Following the scent of food to the kitchen, Heath was stunned to see Kat, hair tied back, sleeves rolled up, standing by the Aga, stirring something in a pan on the hotplate. Her face was flushed from the heat and a large apron was wrapped almost twice around her slender form. The well-worn red cotton did nothing to disguise the feminine appeal of her figure and Heath fought against the sudden raw twist of lust that had him hardening in an instant, the hungry response a mixture of pleasure and pain in almost equal measures.

'So your brother has you cooking for him now,' he questioned in an attempt to hide the kick of his senses.

'Joe's still asleep,' Kat told him, her eyes fixed on the pot she was stirring. 'He's hardly moved at all. But I thought that Harry at least would need something to eat when he gets back from school. I'm making vegetable soup—the veg was all I could find in the larder.'

The curl of her lips and the way she wrinkled her nose

told him how much she disapproved of that. *Men!* she might as well have said.

'I haven't had any time to do any grocery shopping,' he drawled, making it sound as if he didn't care.

He could easily have brought in a team of cleaners and then decorators, to sort out the place, a cook to prepare any meals he wanted, bought brand-new furnishings for every room, but that would be to reveal his hand before he was fully ready to play it. For now he was content to wait and watch, and he would know exactly when the moment to pounce was right.

And that would come soon. Heath smiled lazily, watching the way that Kat's attention was so carefully focused on her cooking. Too focused. Far, far too carefully.

She was fighting to make sure that she didn't look in his direction; struggling to assume an indifference to his presence when all the time her tautly held body, her stiff neck and high, lifted head were like the response of a wary cat faced with an antagonistic intruder into its territory.

'And I have more important things to do than the housekeeping your brother has neglected for the past decade.'

'What? More card games?' The tartness of her response revealed even more than the tension in her spine. 'More fortunes to steal? More lives to ruin?'

Heath's laughter was hard and sharp, brusquely dismissing her anger as an irrelevance.

'My dear Lady Katherine, if you consider this neglected land and a rundown set of buildings as any sort of "fortune" then I believe that we are not thinking along the same lines. And as for stealing—I assure you that I own High Farm fair and square. Everything was above board and legal.'

'Legal maybe but I doubt very much if it was at all fair!'

'The card game was just the last straw. He already owed

me—I gave him a chance to win something back. Are you implying that I cheated?'

The hiss of anger that iced his voice got through to her, bringing her head swinging round, her eyes widening, her soft pink mouth forming a sudden oh of shock.

'Not at all! No! I would never think that. You would never do that.'

The obvious consternation in her voice, the rather wild shake of her head, convinced him of her honesty, soothing the bite of his anger. But with her anxious eyes still fixed on him, her lush mouth still partly open in that way, it was all that he could do just to nod and shrug, as if nothing else were affecting him in any way.

'Smells good...'

An inclination of his head indicated the pot, the wooden spoon she held, frozen above her cooking.

'Would you like some? Or have you eaten?'

'No—I haven't eaten. And yes, I would like some if there is enough to spare.'

'More than enough,' Kat laughed. 'When I make soup, I always make enough to feed an army. Come and sit down.'

She waved a hand in the direction of the battered pine table where bowls and plates were stacked, a bundle of spoons and knives lying beside them.

'It's just about ready.'

It was as he walked across the unevenly tiled floor, heading for the seat she had indicated, that it hit him. A sudden rush of pleasure and longing, and a terrible deep dark emptiness, blended so thoroughly together that he didn't know where one ended and the other began. And they were all so dependent on each other for existence that he couldn't have separated them if he'd tried.

This was how it could have been. The thought slashed into his brain and, once settled there, it wouldn't go away again, burrowing deep into his thoughts like some deadly worm that brought pain with every single move it made.

This was how it might have been if only things had been different. If her father hadn't died. If her brother had never turned into the bitter tyrant who took his hatred of life out on everyone else around him. If she had never been tempted by the luxury and comfort of life at the Grange, the clothes, the jewellery, the money, the position in society. If she had never rejected him and thrown his heart—the heart that had been all he had had to give her—right back in his face.

Once it had been all that he had hoped for. A secret dream that he had kept completely to himself, never believing that it would ever be possible to achieve what he longed for. A house, a place of security and comfort, somewhere to come back to at the end of a long hard day of work. A place where his wife would be, perhaps with a meal prepared, perhaps waiting to share the cooking with him. A wife who would make the house, any house, whether large or small, the home that he had never had all his life. The home he had dreamed of.

And not just any wife but the one woman he had always wanted more than any other. The one woman who could satisfy him, heart, soul and body. The only woman he had truly needed.

Katherine Nicholls now Katherine Charlton. The woman who had turned from him and married one of his most detested enemies.

He had houses now. More than any man needed. Big—huge—houses on almost every continent. Unconsciously his hand crept up to tug at the emerald sparkling in one ear lobe—the vivid, brilliant symbol of the source of his wealth. Just a tiny fragment of all he now possessed. He was rich, powerful beyond all imaginings. But none of the houses he owned was more than a place to live. To eat and sleep. To indulge in the needs of his body, and try to ease his restive mind.

None of the houses he had could ever be described as a home. Certainly not the home he had once dreamed might be his.

Foolishly dreamed, he told himself on a rush of fury that had him pulling out a chair with a raw scraping sound as the wooden legs dragged over the stone-flagged floor. He had never belonged. Had always been, as Joe had described him, the cuckoo in the nest.

This kitchen was the first part of the house he had ever seen. The place where Mr Nicholls had first deposited him when he had brought him, a lost and starving orphan, back from the streets of Liverpool where he had found him. He had been bundled up inside the man's heavy coat, worn as protection against the cold wind and driving rain, and as the three-times-too-big garment was peeled away from him he had found himself the focus of four watching eyes. Kat's dark blue gaze, curious and intrigued, and Joe's cold, hostile pale glare.

'Who the hell is he?' Joe had demanded. 'And what's he doing here?'

'I found him starving and lost on the streets of Liverpool, begging for money to buy food,' his father had said. 'He can barely speak a word of English, and no one there knew anything about him. I'll have to inform the authorities—see what they can do—but I wasn't prepared to leave him there on a night like this. He'll need a hot bath—and go and fetch some of your clothes for him, Joey. He can't wear these stinking things all night.'

'Like hell I will! Why should I give this gipsy beggar anything of mine?'

'Soup…'

Kat had filled a blue pottery bowl with the steaming food and now she set it down on the table in front of him, jolting him back into awareness of the present and out of his memories of the past.

'There's bread in the cupboard. It looks a bit hard but I think if you toast it, it'll be all right.'

'Just the soup will be fine. Thanks.'

Vegetable soup had been the first meal he had ever eaten in this house, too, he reflected. Unlike her brother, Kat had seen how cold and thin he had been and she had turned away silently, coming back to him with a steaming bowlful of soup that she had pushed into his hands. If he was of a fanciful frame of mind, he could have claimed that he had fallen for her right there and then, even if she had only been no more than seven, and he two years younger than Joseph's thirteen.

Picking up a spoon, he dug it into the food then stopped, unable to take the action any further. The memories were there, clogging his throat, making it impossible to eat.

'What the hell is he here for anyway?'

He could almost hear Joe's voice coming back to him across the years.

'He needed help—and I thought that if the authorities allow it we could perhaps adopt him.'

'Adopt him?' It was a sound of pure horror and disgust.

'Yes—you could have a new brother.'

'I don't want a brother! I don't want anything to do with the dirty gipsy scum.'

The look he had turned on Heath was filled with such venom that he had almost felt it should kill him right then and there. And when Joe found that the computer game his father had promised him had fallen out of Mr Nicholls's pocket on the way home and was lost for good, he had stormed out of the room, slamming the door behind him as he went.

'I'll never accept him as my brother—never!' he yelled on his way upstairs. 'And if you've got any sense at all you'll take him back to the slums where he belongs.'

'…take it back…'

'*Que?*'

Dragged back from his memories, Heath reacted without thinking, resorting to the language he had been speaking instead of English for so many years, frowning his confusion as he did so.

'*Desculpe?*'

'I take it all back,' Kat repeated, placing her own bowl on the table and pulling out the chair opposite. 'What I said about you wanting Joe dead. I should never have said it.'

'I've come close enough to it at times.'

He was supposed to eat now—when she was settling into the chair opposite, the scent of her skin reaching over the table towards him, her blue eyes intent on his face, her dark hair falling like a soft cloud over her face as she bent to push her spoon into the soup?

'But you have never actually done anything about it— nor would you, no matter what the provocation. And Joe has been intensely provoking—downright vile at times. You might have wanted to give him a good thrashing but you'd never… Is there something wrong with the soup?'

He had looked keen enough when she had offered him the simple meal, Kat thought. But ever since she had put the bowl down in front of him, it had been as if he was lost in thought, drifting off into some other world. No— that had happened before she'd actually brought the soup over, she realised. From the moment he'd sat down, he'd been absorbed in some private reflection. And one that

wasn't at all happy if the frown that had drawn his dark
brows together had been anything to go by.

'No, nothing...'

Heath's response was abstracted, vague. His attempt
at a polite smile—if that was what it was—was nothing
more than a half-hearted curl at the corner of his lips.

'I was waiting for it to cool.'

'If you wait much longer then it will be cold!'

She aimed for flippancy but found that her tone missed
a bit, slipping into the aching sadness of memory that suddenly had her in its grip as she tried to concentrate on her
cooking. Seeing Heath here, like this, in such once-famil-
iar surroundings, in the kitchen that had been so much
part of their growing up, it was so very hard not to let her
thoughts dwell on memories of past times.

'You weren't so hesitant that first time I ever gave you
soup,' she managed, though her voice shook slightly on
the words.

The day he had first arrived in her life, brought home
by her father from Liverpool, a dark, scruffy, dirty-faced
urchin with barely a word or two of English in his vocab-
ulary. A boy who had looked so wild, so fiercely defiant
and yet who had some terrible sense of loss and loneliness underneath the determined mask he had shown to
the world. Unlike her brother, who had flown into a savage rage at just the thought of having this stranger in the
house, she had wanted to show him that he was welcome.
But, unable to understand whatever language it was that he
spoke, she had resorted to the wordless gesture of fetching
him something to eat. A bowl of soup, she remembered.
Made to exactly this same recipe.

'I'd have eaten a piece of coal if that was what you had
offered me,' Heath acknowledged on a rueful laugh. 'You
were the first person other than your father to offer me

help. Unlike Joe who was glaring at me as if looks could kill.'

'I think he saw you as a rival to my father's affections. They always had a rather—difficult relationship.'

'And he felt I was the cuckoo in the nest.'

'You certainly seemed like some sort of alien that day.'

Kat knew she was really only talking to fill the silence and yet at the same time she was trying to find some way to claim back the Heath she had once known. The boy who had been her friend and not this coldly distant stranger. It was ironic to think that she had once wished he would smarten himself up, do something with his life, and now here he was the perfect example of what she had wanted for him and those changes had altered him completely. The table between them might be an enormous, unbridgeable chasm, they were now so desperately far apart. And yet, for herself, she had never been so stunningly aware of him in the most feminine, sensual ways.

'No one could understand a word you were saying. It took us ages to discover that you were actually speaking Portuguese.'

Realisation suddenly dawned and her spoon actually dropped back into the bowl as she stared at him.

'That was why you went to Brazil?'

Heath inclined his head in agreement as he stirred his spoon round in the still steaming soup.

'I wanted to see if I could track any family. I had small clues—my mother who brought me to England then abandoned me when she realised that no man would look after her with a small boy in tow.'

Kat flinched to hear him recount the story of how he had come to be wandering the streets of Liverpool on his own even though she had heard it before, when he had finally learned enough English to explain it. Social services had brought in a native Portuguese speaker and had tried to track down Heath's missing family, but they had never succeeded and eventually her father had adopted him.

His hand went up to tug at the emerald in his ear lobe as if touching some talisman that connected him with his past and something in the gesture pulled at her heart. She had never been able to understand how any mother could abandon her child alone in a foreign country. Her heart had bled for the little boy Heath had been when she had first heard of it and it ached for him still now. Impulsively she reached out a hand, meaning to touch Heath's fingers, in a very different way from the sensual impulse she had felt earlier. But one quick, flashing glance from those ebony eyes had her freezing and then pulling back, warned off by that look, no words needing to be spoken. Now it was her turn to focus on stirring her spoon round in her soup.

'And did you? Find anyone?'

'I found my father.'

'And was he the Emperor of China? Or Brazil at least.'

It raised a small smile, a quirk of his lips, in recognition of their old joke. But he shook his head.

'He is a wealthy, powerful man. He owns several mines in Minas Gerais. I actually took a job with him before I discovered who he was.'

'Heath Montanha…'

'That, apparently, is my family name.'

'So that's where your wealth—no?' Kat questioned as Heath shook his dark head again.

'I was only one of many bastard sons he had fathered on several women he had as mistresses. And from what I learned, he was never too concerned about his parental responsibilities. That must have been why my mother left him and came to England in the first place. My money I made myself. While my father might mine for topaz and aquamarine, I found a rich deposit of emeralds...'

Again his fingers touched the jewel in his ear.

'The Itabira mine. This was the first stone I ever excavated from there.'

'It's beautiful.'

Kat's response was vague, abstracted. There was something fretting at the back of her mind, like an itch that she couldn't quite scratch. Something she should remember, something important. But she couldn't quite place it.

'You've come a long way since we were all kids sitting round this table for meals.'

'I could say the same about you. But this kitchen hasn't changed all that much from the moment we first met.'

And the day he had left. The last time she had ever seen him they had been in here too. He had snarled at her when she had reproached him for being rude to her visiting friends—Arthur Charlton and others.

'*We* were supposed to be friends,' he had growled. 'But you seem to have forgotten that. Take a look at the calendar—see the dates you've marked to go out with your new-found "friends". The number of nights you're away, staying over at the Grange, going to clubs ...'

'I'm entitled to some fun,' she had tried to reason, only to be dealt a glare of such total contempt that she felt as if it had flayed a protective layer of skin from her body, leaving her painfully raw and vulnerable, and resentful of the way he managed to make her uncomfortable in this way. 'I can't always be staying at home with you. You're always in such a foul mood—you have nothing to talk about.'

'Of course,' Heath had scorned. 'It is so much *fun* to be with Arthur Charlton who will be an earl one day and who has a fortune at his back. And do you ever wonder why I am in such a foul mood?'

'Because you're jealous?' she had flashed back. 'Because you have to stay and work instead of enjoying yourself the way we do.'

'If you think that,' he had said slowly and forcefully, dark fury blazing in his eyes, setting his jaw tight and hard, 'then you really don't know me at all.'

'You know what? Perhaps I don't know you—you're not the person you used to be. In fact, the way you are now, I'm not even sure I *want* to know you.'

Those were the last words she had spoken to him. That night he had packed his belongings and walked out, leaving without goodbyes or explanations. He had turned his back on her and rejected everything there had ever been between them.

'Even the soup's the same. Does—doesn't it taste good?' she tried now, knowing that the memory of that rejection was what made her tongue stumble over the words.

That and the new, disturbing sensations that simply sitting opposite him, looking into his dark, shuttered face were sparking off inside her body. She'd tried to ease the feeling by dropping her gaze to his hands where one held the spoon, the other lying flat on the table beside the bowl. But seeing the long, bronze-skinned fingers, all she could think of was the pleasure of having those hands touch her, skin to skin, hard palms against the softness of her flesh. Her own hands twitched with the need to reach out and make contact, trace the strong bones, the tight muscles, and just the thought of that connection made a melting heat form low down in her body.

She had never felt like this with Arthur. She had always assumed that passion would grow from the warmth and friendship she had thought they had shared. She couldn't have been more wrong. With her husband she had tried everything, silk dresses, fine perfumes, creams to soften her skin. But nothing had made any difference. Nothing had made Arthur want her as she had needed—longed to be wanted. And nothing had made her feel as she did now, dressed only in old jeans and a well-worn sweater. In Heath's presence she felt all woman, devastatingly aware of her body, of her femininity. He only had to look at her to make her feel as if she were on fire.

'It's fine.'

Obviously meaning to appease her anxiety, he took a large spoonful and swallowed it down. His reaction was unexpected, his sudden smile knocking her off balance.

'What are you smiling at?'

'It's good.'

'And this makes you smile because?'

'Because I never expected that you would turn out to have any domestic skills—or any interest at all in cooking.'

'I was fifteen!'

'And don't I know it!'

It was said with such emphasis, such a cynical intonation that it stopped her thoughts dead, made her stare at him in confusion.

'You were fifteen and I was nearly nineteen,' he said as if that explained it. That dark undertone was still there, making the comment a whole lot more than a simple statement of fact.

'So...' She began but at that moment a noise from upstairs, the sound of Joe on his feet and moving unsteadily around, distracted her and pushed her up from her chair in a rush. 'I'd better go and make sure that he doesn't fall over. Perhaps some soup will help to sober him up and bring him round a bit.'

The task of sorting out her brother took far longer than she had anticipated because although awake he was still far from fully sober, his mood awkward and recalcitrant. So she wasn't able to return downstairs for some time. When she did it was to find that Heath had finished his soup, cleared the bowl and spoon to the sink where he had washed it and was now drying it before putting it away.

'Will you need to collect Harry from school?' he asked as she came into the room, nodding his head towards the clock on the wall.

Startled, she registered the time, and faced the realisation that she was never going to be able to get to the school before Harry came out.

'I can't get him in time. I'd have to go back and fetch the car.'

'You didn't drive here?'

'No, I walked. I—needed some air.'

She couldn't meet his eyes as she answered. Would the memories be in his face too? she wondered. The recollection of how many times they had shared that walk from the village to the farm together, thinking nothing of the three miles distance, enjoying the freedom and the wildness of the moors. Enjoying being together.

'Then I can give you a lift in my car.'

'That would be kind. And you're right, I should be leaving soon. But why would you want to help…?'

'My reasons are the same as the ones for taking him to school in the first place—someone needs to do it.'

'But he's Joe's son. The son of the man you hate…'

'And we have been through this before. I have no intention of hurting your nephew. He is a child. He is innocent in all this'

'But if you turf my brother out into the streets…'

'Did I say that I intended to do that?' Heath questioned smoothly.

'I assumed…'

'Do not make assumptions. You will be wrong, Lady Katherine.'

Was that a statement or a threat? She didn't know how to interpret it and Heath's expression was giving her no help, his eyes hooded and hidden. He had tossed down the tea towel now and was staring out of the window, watching the heavy rain clouds that were being swept towards the house by the strong winds that had got up during the afternoon.

'So what did you have planned, then?'

'Planned?' Heath shrugged negligently, the gesture expressing supreme indifference. 'I can't say I have thought that through.'

Now that, Kat refused to believe. If there was one thing that she had learned about this new Heath who had come back into her life, it was that he thought everything through. Thoroughly and completely. She had only to look into his face, to see the gleam in his dark eyes, the calculating look, to know that he was totally in control of every move, every word.

'If you really do own the farm…'

'Which I do.'

'Then Joe will have nothing. No home. No job.'

And I should care? One slow flick of those thick black lashes was all that it took to express the comment without words.

'I would be perfectly happy to offer him a post.'

A carefully calculated pause told her that there was more to come and that all she could do was to wait for him to finish.

'Perhaps as a pigman…?'

It sounded so innocent. So open and straightforward. But Kat could be in no doubt that he knew exactly what he was doing. He knew how much Joe would hate the job— hate any job Heath offered simply because it put him in the position of being a subordinate to the man who had already ruined his life and now held his entire wealth very firmly in his hands.

'It would come with accommodation.' Heath held her eyes with his and she knew exactly what was coming. 'I believe my bed is still in the shed outside.'

'You can't put anyone in that dump. It's cruel—inhuman...'

Her voice trailed away as she saw the look on his face, remembered how he had spent months sleeping in just that same dump.

'I was always surprised that you stayed there. I felt sure you'd just walk out.'

'Believe me, I wanted to.'

'So why didn't you?'

'If you have to ask that question then it doesn't merit a reply.'

It was obvious that Heath wasn't going to provide her with any more of an answer. He was reaching for his jacket, shrugging it on. The conversation was at an end and there was nothing she could do to revive it. Heath jerked his chin towards the door and his car parked beyond it.

'If you want to collect Harry, we should leave now.'

The journey to the school was fast and comfortable in Heath's sleek, powerful car but with Kat's mind still in turmoil, working through their earlier conversation, she barely noticed the miles pass until they drew up outside the school gates.

'Where will you take him?' Heath asked as he switched

off the engine and leaned back in his seat. Kat's silence
on the journey was obviously because she still worried
that he would harm her nephew. If only she knew that the
truth was the exact opposite. The boy reminded him too
much of his own self at that age. A little better fed perhaps, but the sense of loss was so much the same. Harry's
father was as absent as his own parents had been, even if
he was technically in the boy's life.

'You can hardly take him back to High Farm with his
father out of it like that.'

'You're right.'

She nodded slowly, watching as the school door opened,
her eyes searching for her nephew in the wave of children
who rushed out of the building.

'And when the farm is actually no longer his home,'
she added pointedly.

If the reproach was meant to sting then it did, making
his hands clench tightly on the steering wheel so that she
turned to glance at him swiftly, her eyes cold and withdrawn.

'If you are throwing Joe out then you'll be doing the
same to his son. They come as a pair. Get rid of Joe and
you put Harry out of the only home he's ever known. I
can't believe that you would want to do that.'

'I told you not to make assumptions.'

He just wished she'd let the subject drop. All these demands were making him face queries he didn't have an
explanation for. Questions he couldn't even answer for
himself.

'You're not going to throw him out?'

He pushed a hand through his hair, noting that her
nephew had appeared in the doorway. A small, dark-haired
figure, much the same age as he had been when Kat's fa-

ther had rescued him from the streets of Liverpool and brought him home with him.

It made him pause, made him think. This boy was the son of the man he had come here to ruin. The man he had spent a lifetime hating and on whom he had vowed to have his revenge. It was what he had come here for. But somewhere along the line things had changed.

'As far as I'm concerned, Joe can rot in hell and I'll happily pile on some extra coals just to keep it nice and hot—but Harry is a different matter.'

And as Harry dashed across the playground towards the car, a wide brilliant smile breaking out as he saw his aunt, Heath suddenly felt the shock of recognition he'd known earlier, felt the knots he had spent all day trying to ease from his stomach form once again and tighten mercilessly. And it was so much worse because of the woman who was sitting beside him, leaning forward now to wave towards her nephew.

The movement brought her neat behind so close that it was pressing into his thigh, the warmth of her body reaching through the denim to his own skin. The smooth, straight line of her back, the curve of her hip, the fall of dark hair that she now tossed back out of her face all tugged on sensual urges he had been fighting to control. Her perfume seemed to pervade the air inside the car, swirling round him like warm smoke, teasing his senses, blurring his eyes, thickening in his throat.

He wanted to look away, to look anywhere but at her. Anything to distract himself from the pounding in his head, the meltdown in his blood. His jeans were too tight where his body had reacted in heat and hardness to every feminine signal she was giving off and he had to shift uncomfortably in his seat to try and ease the pressure. He needed to look somewhere else, anywhere else, to divert his attention from the overwhelming awareness that she was a woman and he was a man. A man who wanted this woman, hungered for her more than he had ever craved any woman in his past.

But it was when he stared out of the car, focusing his gaze out through the windscreen and beyond, that he looked straight into Harry's smiling face and knew once again the shock of recognition that had assailed him that morning. There was no point in even trying to deny it to himself any longer. When he looked into the child's eyes he saw Kat's eyes, the same deep dark blue that marked them out as aunt and nephew. In Harry's innocent gaze he saw the Kat he had known, and loved from his own childhood, through the turmoil and torment of his adolescence. And that was why he would always have a weakness where the little boy was concerned, no matter who or what his father might be.

'How could I do that to Harry?' he growled. 'How can I leave him homeless and bereft? I've been there. I've lived through it twice and I would never willingly inflict it on any kid.'

Kat half turned in her seat, looking at him with wide, stunned eyes. The same eyes that he had just acknowledged as the weakness he could damn well do without. And the dawning smile at the back of them only made things so much worse.

'You mean…?'

'I mean that your brother can stay where he is until he has somewhere to go. I don't need that room—not until I start work on bringing the place into some kind of order. So he can sleep there for now—but as soon as he finds somewhere…'

Harry was with them now, tumbling into the car and into his aunt's hug with a flurry of movement and chatter and they had to drop the conversation, change it to something more suitable. But not before Kat had turned to him one more time and mouthed a silent and heartfelt, 'Thank you,' over her nephew's dark head.

'So now where?'

He could do nothing about the gruffness of his voice but at least the need to switch on the engine, get the car into gear gave him something else to concentrate on and direct his attention to focus on the road ahead. He had to get a grip on himself or he would be in no fit state to drive, with his concentration shot to pieces.

'Do you want to go back to the Grange?'

He didn't even flick a glance in her direction, not wanting to heat his blood again after he had fought to get it at least that tiny bit cooler. One look would set his heart pounding, his body yearning for what it could not have.

At least not now. Not yet. Not unless he broke his vow to himself that he would wait.

'Yes, please.'

She sounded almost formally polite as if something of his mood had rubbed off on her, making her stiff and awkward for fear of letting out things she never wanted him to know.

'That is, if it's all right for you.'

It would be all right if it killed him. But as he steered the car way from the kerb and headed in the direction of the road to Hawden, he suddenly remembered the way that Isobel had been so blatantly flirtatious with him on his arrival there. He knew that look. The way a woman reacted when she had set her sights on him.

He'd also seen the flash of something in Kat's eyes when he had turned his attention to the other woman. Something close to jealousy. Though she'd deny it with the last breath in her body of course. But he could use that rivalry to his own advantage.

'That will suit me fine,' he said more easily, smiling to himself as he put his foot down on the accelerator.

CHAPTER SIX

'HEATH says that he's just taking me to lunch in Leeds, but I'm sure I can persuade him to do a little shopping too.'

Isobel smiled like the Cheshire cat that had just been presented with a particularly delicious bowl of cream as she announced her plans.

'And get him to spend an inordinate amount of money on me.'

Her smile was wide and bright and she waggled her eyebrows with exaggerated enthusiasm.

'I mean—he's seriously loaded, isn't he?'

Kat managed to make some non-committal murmur that Isobel could take for agreement if she wanted to. She had had enough of the way that her sister-in-law flaunted her fascination with Heath in her face and she was quite frankly tired of hearing just how much his obvious wealth was an important part of his appeal.

'Belle, are you sure that you're being sensible?'

'Sensible?' her sister-in-law laughed. 'Sensible is for old fogeys like you. I'm only twenty and I want to have some fun.'

'And you think that's what Heath wants too?'

'Of course!'

Isobel rolled her eyes in exasperation at Kat's tone,

shaking her head so that her blonde hair swung out around her face.

'If I could just get him to see that I'm the person he wants to have fun with.'

'But are you sure you know what you're doing? Like you say, Heath isn't the sort of man you're used to. He's so much older than you and he's...'

Dangerous was the word that sprang to mind. Threatening. Hidden. Enigmatic. She knew that if Isobel challenged her she would be hard put to explain those feelings. To her sister-in-law he was charm itself.

Lethal was another. But that meant lethal to her sense of equilibrium. Lethal to her peace of mind. Just being in the same room as him knocked her right off balance and had the world hazing round her.

'Oh, I grant you there's a real age gap. He is pretty old,' Isobel said, with blithe disregard for that fact that at barely thirty Heath was a man very much in his prime. 'But he is really hot—*hot*!'

She fanned a hand in front of her face as if trying to cool herself down.

'And he's all man!'

'Are you saying...?'

Kat caught herself up sharply, shocked at the way that she had jumped on Isobel's words. She was appalled that it mattered to her so much.

'Oh, we haven't even kissed yet!' Isobel laughed. 'Though it's not for want of trying—on my part anyway! Do you know, if it wasn't for the fact that he's so blatantly hetero, I might actually have worried that he was gay. But he isn't—he just couldn't be.'

Unconsciously Kat's hand slipped up to touch on her mouth, tracing the line of her lips, the soft flesh that had once been crushed so fiercely by Heath's kiss.

Remembering that moment and the hard, hot evidence of the fact that he had been so strongly aroused, she could be in no doubt at all that Heath was as straight as they came. It was shocking to find that just recalling it made her blood burn in her veins, setting a pulse throbbing between her legs. Even in bed with Arthur, when he had kissed her, touched her, she had never felt that. She had tried. She had really believed that she could make it work with her husband, but he had never truly wanted her. Or any woman, it seemed, considering where he had been found on the night he'd died.

In bed with another man, with his body pumped full of heroin.

Something cold and slimy seemed to slide down her spine as her memory threw at her the image of long, miserable nights in Arthur's bed. Nights when she had tried to get him to consummate their marriage only to have his failure to achieve an erection thrown in her face with the vicious accusation that *she* was frigid, sexless—not a real woman. And not knowing anything else, she had believed him. But if there was anything she needed to prove to her that their failed sexual relationship had been Arthur's problem and not hers, then the way she responded to Heath, to his kisses, the heated erotic dreams that had started to plague her nights, had given her proof of that.

I know what's wrong with you! Her husband's voice echoed through the clinging tendrils of unhappiness, his words raw with anger and accusation. *You're not interested in a gentleman! You're still dreaming of your bit of rough—that gipsy. That's what turns you on.*

And to her total consternation, it seemed that he was right.

'Of course I'm joking.'

Preening in front of the mirror, hands fluffing up her

blonde hair, Isobel was oblivious of Kat's silence, her sudden withdrawal from the conversation. 'He's obviously straight—but I've been giving him the green light for *weeks* now and he's—you don't think he's not interested, do you?'

Just for a moment her light blue eyes, so like her brother's, flicked to Kat's face in the mirror, a questioning frown bringing together her fair brows.

'No!' she answered for herself, not caring that Kat couldn't quite form the words to respond. 'No chance. Perhaps he's just playing the gentlemen—him being a gipsy, and me the daughter of an earl. Well, whatever I am, I'm all woman...'

Smoothing her hands down over her voluptuous curves, she gave a small shimmy of delight, smiling her satisfaction at her appearance as she did so.

'And, I'm going to get him to take me out to dinner tonight—and then *Senhor* gipsy Heath is not going to know what hit him. I have a gor-ge-ous...' she dragged out each syllable with almost lascivious relish '...new dress—just wait till he gets an eyeful of that. It's slit down to here...'

But Kat had had as much as she could take.

'Belle—stop—please! Too much information.'

'Oh, sorry, Kat.'

Instantly Isobel was all contrition.

'I should have thought. Obviously you're feeling frustrated too. After all it's more than a year now since you had...'

And that was just too much. The thought that her sister-in-law might think she was actually missing her husband physically—that she had any physical relationship to miss—almost pushed Kat over the edge.

'Enough, Belle! *Enough!*'

She didn't know whether she wanted to scream or rage

or cry or do all three at once but luckily at that moment she was saved from having to do anything by the sound of the doorbell. One sharp ring summoned her, but before she had time even to reach the hall the door had opened and the subject of her thoughts, Heath himself, strolled into the room, bringing her up short.

It brought her up short emotionally as well. With the whirling confusion of her thoughts still leaving her struggling, she was ill-prepared for his appearance, unable to think at all how to react. So she jumped into the one thing she probably should have avoided like the plague—revealing just how off balance she was and the way that his arrival had made her feel worse.

'Good morning, Mr Montanha. How nice to see you.'

The bite of acid in that 'nice' made it only too plain that that was not the way she was feeling.

'But tell me, is it normal practice in Brazil simply to walk into someone's house without waiting for them to come to the door?'

'*Bom dia* to you too, Lady Katherine.' Heath's rich drawl was touched with dark humour and the wicked gleam in the black depths of his eyes taunted her with the secret of something that he knew and that she strongly suspected she was very soon to find out.

She was right.

'I told Heath to just walk in,' Isobel put in from behind her. 'After all, we're friends now...'

She sauntered past Kat, holding out her arms to Heath, lifting her face to be kissed.

'Aren't we, darling?'

'Of course.'

He bent to give her the kiss she wanted, but on her cheek, not the pouting mouth she so obviously meant him to caress. That way his dark eyes could still hold Kat's stunned blue ones and she saw the way that the glow of dark amusement flared for a moment as he watched her expression change.

'Isobel's friends are always welcome,' Kat jumped in sharply, putting the careful emphasis on that 'Isobel's' in the hope that her foolish mind—and even more foolish emotions—would actually believe it. She had to fight to control the way the thudding of her heart brought the blood rushing to her cheeks, her pulse seeming to skip a beat, almost turning somersaults inside as she tried to face down that mocking smile.

'You bet they are,' giggled her sister-in-law, linking her arms through Heath's and cuddling close, pressing the length of her body along the side of his.

'Especially when they offer lunch at Quatro's, hmm?' Heath put in, his tone apparently light, but with an unexpected edge that caught Kat on the raw.

Her skin shivered at the sound, but she couldn't make out whether it was because of the tone of the words or the contrast between them and the black ice that was in his eyes. A coldness that in no way matched the teasing intonation and made her stomach twist sharply at the thought that Isobel was too excited by his comment to see what lay behind it.

'Quatro's? You mean it…? Kat, did you hear that? We're having lunch at Quatro's.'

'I heard.' She couldn't put any emotion into it, try as she might.

'Go and fetch your coat,' Heath instructed. 'It's cold outside.'

'I won't be a minute—but first I'm going to have to change into something different. I'm really not dressed for lunch at Quatro's!'

Kat waited until Isobel had run up the stairs, heading

for her room. Then she turned to Heath, eyes sparking
with challenge.

'What are you doing with Isobel?'

'Doing?'

Heath's appearance was pure innocence, so obviously
assumed that her fingers itched to wipe the lying expression from his face.

'I am taking your sister-in-law on a trip to Leeds.'

'Not that...'

An impatient wave of her hand dismissed the blatantly
deliberate lack of understanding of what she meant.

'I mean what you are *doing* with her—long term—
or...?'

The words shrivelled on her tongue as she saw the dark
frown that snapped his black brows together over his blazing eyes, the sudden ferocity of his anger shaking her.

'What is this, Lady Katherine? Do you think that I
should explain my intentions? Or perhaps you need me to
tell you of my prospects so that you can decide whether I
am fit to be seen with your sister-in-law?'

'Oh, don't be ridiculous!'

'Ridiculous?'

The way he echoed the word, putting a vicious emphasis on it, made her flinch away inside.

'Ridiculous,' he repeated. 'Is that what I am? So tell
me—what is it to you if I want to see Isobel?'

'I just wanted to know what you are doing...'

'That is my business.'

'And mine. I promised Arthur I'd look after her.'

No, the mention of her husband had been a mistake.
Dark fire flashed even more savagely in those ebony eyes,
making her wish she'd never started this.

'She—she's my sister-in-law.'

'And a grown woman.'

'She's barely twenty.'

'I was out in the world, making my own living, fending totally for myself when I was almost two years younger than she is now,' Heath pointed out.

And he had been because of her family. Because her brother had thrown him out of the house and because Heath's name had been blacklisted and her husband had made sure that he couldn't get any employment anywhere in the area. The accusation was there whether he had stated it or not. And it was one she couldn't deny.

'But she's innocent...'

The cynical quirking up of one black brow, questioning the accuracy of that statement, almost finished her but she had to force herself to go on.

'She thinks she knows it all but really she's desperately naïve. She's lived such a sheltered life here—and at boarding school.'

'And you think that I am not fit to associate with your delicately brought up little sister-in-law?'

'No—' Kat tried to protest. 'It's not like that. It's...'

'It's what?' Heath snapped out the question. 'The truth, my dear Katherine, is that it's nothing to do with you. Nothing. I have a right to spend time with her if she chooses. And you have no right to object.'

'No—'

Looking into Heath's face, seeing the bronzed skin, the slash of high, carved cheekbones, the jet-dark burn of those deep-set eyes, she felt alternately as if she were in the grip of a burning fever or the cruel grip of ice. Ice that melted into a pool of heated honey leaving her struggling to find any words to answer him.

'So is it that your well-bred husband will be spinning in the grave at the thought that a mere gipsy might have his dirty hands on a member of his illustrious family?'

'I never called you a gipsy!'

'True,' Heath acknowledged roughly. 'You were the one person who never used that description of me. But if you had then you would have been right, *querida*—because that is exactly what I am. My mother at least was a gipsy, born and bred. That is why my father never married her— why she travelled to England to look for some other members of her family, but ended up, lost and penniless on the streets of Liverpool.'

'I never thought of you like that.'

'So what upsets *you* so much if I spend a little time with your sister-in-law?'

His mouth curled around the words as if they were some foul-tasting medicine that was poisoning his whole system and she could see the burn of bitter memory in the darkness of his eyes.

'Could you possibly be jealous, *carina*?'

'Jealous!'

Even in her own ears her voice sounded too shrill, too harsh to be convincing. And she knew that this time her laughter was way off the mark. For the first time since the awkward, uncomfortable conversation had begun she wished that Isobel would hurry up and come back downstairs. But she knew that once her sister-in-law decided to change her clothes, and was trying to select the best possible outfit, she could be a long time making up her mind.

'You have to be joking.'

She tried to look away, out of the window, up the stairs, anywhere, but she couldn't move. Those burning eyes held her transfixed. She felt that they could reach inside her, open her soul, and take out every last secret she had ever held.

'No joke.'

He muttered something in his native language—or

rather the language he had acquired from living in Brazil, with his father. She couldn't take her eyes from his sensual mouth as it formed the words, the memory of the taste of those lips against her own making her slick her tongue along her own mouth as if they were still there.

'What? What are you saying?'

His smile frightened her, making her stomach clench in tight response.

'I said that I think you are a liar—but a very beautiful one.'

'Beautiful...'

Her tongue formed the word without her volition, drawing it out into a sigh, and she saw the flare of aroused response in those ebony eyes that flickered over her for a moment, and then stilled again, his gaze resting like a caress at her lips. Did he know how it made her feel to be told that she was beautiful for the first time in her life? What a balm that was to the soul, the self-esteem, that her husband had lacerated so often with his cruelty, his scorn? So much so that it seemed to drain all the strength from her, stopping her from fighting as she needed to.

Somehow she pulled herself together, dragging her mind away from the hypnotic effect he seemed to be weaving around her.

'I'm not lying!' she declared, desperate to distract herself—and him.

Once more a lifted eyebrow questioned the truth of her assertion and she found herself shaking her head frantically, needing to deny the query that teased over her skin.

'I am not a liar,' she repeated as coldly and as clearly as she could manage.

'Really?'

It was that slow compelling drawl that reached out and caught her in its net, tugging tight with a slow, steady pull.

'And would you care to prove that?'

'Yes—' Or did she mean, 'No…'?

She didn't know which to say and neither of them seemed to have any effect. Her voice had lost all its strength and the word was like a tiny, ineffectual push at his chest, barely making contact and of no use at all in trying to get him to move away.

And he was moving, she realised hazily. She hadn't noticed him take action but he was coming closer, slowly, steadily, almost imperceptibly. He was taking one step and then another, and another…

She should back away, get out of his reach. She told herself that she *wanted* to back away, but her body refused to obey her. Instead she stayed exactly where she was, feet firmly rooted to the ground, her breathing fast and shallow, her heart thudding heavily inside her chest.

'Now how shall we do this, *namorada*?'

'We…?'

We won't be doing it at all, she meant to say, but the single syllable was all she could manage. It seemed that as she spoke she took in the scent of him on the air, her mouth remembered the taste of him and wanted more.

'We…' she said again and it was just a sigh.

'We…' Heath agreed, nodding his dark head. 'Because it is "we", isn't it, my lovely? It is the two of us. Not just you or me—but the two of us together. We.'

The last word was spoken as his head lowered to hers, his mouth taking hers so that she swayed against him, hunger weakening every limb so that she needed his strength to hold and support her as she melted into him.

Three kisses. They had shared only three kisses in all the time she had known him, and yet each kiss had been so very different, so unique, so totally unlike each other that Kat felt as if she had experienced a lifetime of caresses from this man.

The first, here in this hallway on the day he had come back into her life, his kiss had been like being in the eye of a burning storm. The flaring passion had taken her and dropped her right into the heart of an inferno where she had thought that she would be burned up to ashes before her heart could even take another beat. Then the slow seduction of that second had melted her senses, leaving her half out of her mind with the sort of sensual awakening that had filled her whole body with hunger and yearning.

But this kiss was another new experience. And even as his mouth touched hers she knew that this was the kiss that had the potential to break her heart. It was the kiss she had dreamed of, longed for. The kiss she had been waiting for all her life.

Kissing Arthur—and being kissed by him—had been like kissing an enthusiastic boy, clumsy, endearing, excited, but somehow lacking in finesse. She had thought it was just the start of things. That it was bound to get better, but instead it had come to lack even more—but lacking what, she had never known until now. She had taken the blame for it because she hadn't known any better. Until that first kiss from Heath had shown her how it could be between a man and a woman.

How a man should kiss a woman.

This was a man's kiss. And she received it as a woman, knowing that the feelings it stirred in her were the richest, deepest, most feminine emotions possible. It was a kiss that opened her mind and her senses to new sensations: to heat of skin, the scent of his body, the strength of taut muscle, and the taste of his mouth on her, hard and soft in the same moment, moist and warm and totally personal.

To the heat that whirled along every vein, every nerve, stinging them awake and demanding.

Suddenly kissing was not enough. She wanted more. Needed so much more. She wanted to touch, her hands going out to grab at his arms, fingers tightening into the taut muscle under the fine cotton of his shirt. The heat of his skin was only blood warm but it felt as if it seared into her palms, branding her, making her his without hope of redemption. She needed that heat everywhere, on her hands, on her lips, on her body. She couldn't get close enough, crushing herself up against him, the tips of her breasts pressed against the hard cage of his ribs, her hips cradled in his pelvis. The feel of the hardness of him there against the spot where her own body ached for him was something that made her head swim. She knew a tugging sense of fear at the force of it all, of exhilaration at the thought that this could actually be happening. And a glorious, soaring feeling of triumph to know that she could spark off such excitement in any man—let alone a man like Heath.

It was balm to the wounds that Arthur's furious, bitter rejection of her had created, a delight that wiped out the savage disappointment she had experienced in her married life. When Heath's hard hands swept over her body, smoothing the curves of her hips, curling around her waist to bring her even closer she found that she was gasping aloud, breathing her excitement right between his lips. She wanted more from his kiss and leaning forward she took it for herself, letting her tongue dance into his mouth, tangle with his in the delicious provocation of intimacy.

His response was to loose the groan she suspected he had been fighting to hold back, and those searching hands moved up, harder, higher. They curved around the undersides of her breasts, cupping the soft weight and bringing it up, closer than ever, supported in the heat of his palms. His thumbs brushed against the straining tips of her nipples, teasing, knowing, provoking. Arousing sensation that shot like arrows of fire from the tingling peaks straight to the heart of her, the heated, moist core that pulsed between her legs.

So this was what it was all about. Somehow the thought formed, hazy and stunning, in the hot mist that smoked through her thoughts. This was what people made such a fuss about, sex. Why it was talked about in such knowing voices, with such meaningful looks.

She felt as if at last, at almost twenty-five, she had finally awoken. As if, like Sleeping Beauty, she had woken from her trance-like sleep. She had been kissed, not by some handsome prince who would carry her away on a snowy white charger, but by Heath, the boy who had once been her friend but had walked out of her life and had come back as someone else. A gipsy as he had acknowledged for himself, but also a very different man. A man who had been tested and shaped by life, tempered by the harshness of reality, and had come back hardened with a new, primitive dark strength that had ripped open the defences she had thought she'd built around herself and gone straight to the hidden vulnerable heart beneath.

And like Pandora when she had opened the box the gods had given her, letting fly all the wild unknown, unexplored and incomprehensible emotions out into the world, she knew she hadn't a hope in hell of getting them back into containment ever again.

Not that she wanted to. She welcomed these new and exciting feelings. And the hunger that they stirred in her.

But then the sound of a door banging upstairs broke into the heated delirium that filled her mind. The sound of perilously high stiletto heels tapping along the landing warned that Isobel was coming.

The noise had the effect of a slap in the face for Kat. She froze, jerking back instinctively as she fought down the wicked, carnal impulses that had her body screaming a protest.

Isobel was coming. Her sister-in-law, who was happily looking forward to a lunch with this man who had just made a move on her under the pretence of proving that she was jealous.

Was she jealous?

How could she be jealous when she was so appalled at the thought of what had just happened that her body was trembling with the force of her feelings? And worse, how could she have let this happen? How could she have let Heath work his sexual enticement—his lying, cheating, sexual enticement—on her when it was obvious that he felt nothing at all?

The glory of all she had discovered about the truth of being a woman shattered all around her as she faced the fact that she had let her desperation, her need for reassurance, leave her totally vulnerable, at the mercy of a man who was quite capable of using them for his own ends.

'No!'

It was a desperately hissed undertone, determination that Isobel would not hear roughening her voice and strangely, shockingly, making the denial sound more like a husky come-on than the forceful rejection she aimed for. And hearing it Heath simply smiled a devil's smile.

'Liar,' he murmured as he brought his head down towards hers again.

'I said no!'

Afraid that she would not be able to find the strength to resist him again, Kat lifted a hand to push him away as forcefully as possible. But either he had come closer than she had expected or she had lashed out with more force than she had anticipated, because her hand came up against his lean cheek in a slap that made her palm sting, the sickening sound of flesh hitting flesh echoing shockingly in the sudden, frightening silence.

Heath stilled instantly. His whole body stiffened, each muscle taut, and the only hint of emotion she could see was the sudden flare of wild anger in his eyes before he lowered his lids, closing them off, hiding everything behind the fall of the long, lustrous black lashes.

The worrying silence lengthened, dragging out, stretching her nerves with it until she felt that they might snap under the tension they were being subjected to. She could almost feel the battle that Heath was having with himself, the determination not to respond in kind, but the force that held every muscle taut and still. The countdown in his mind, probably going up to ten and then twenty and even more. He still held her, but she could feel his withdrawal in every fingertip, the distance that said the heated, sensual mood of just moments before had gone completely, blasted into a million tiny fragments, impossible ever to put back together again.

And the terrible trouble was that as soon as she had ended it she wished she hadn't. That she wanted it all back again. That glorious rush of sensuality. The feeling of being close and wanted. The sensation of really coming alive after all this time. But most of all the person inside herself that she had just found existed.

She wanted that back and she wanted Heath back. The Heath she had just newly discovered. The man who was not the boy she had once known but had all the power and strength, the sheer presence that she had always known deep down on the most basic, most primal level that Heath would inevitably grow into.

And then at last Heath moved, startling her into wide-eyed shock as she flinched back then caught herself up again. The way he snatched his hands away from her arms, stepping back, and his black frown told her that he would not hurt her, that he was even more angry that she would think so. Somehow that made everything so much worse because it ripped away the defence of physical fear and left her raw and wide open to the only other possibility.

And that was that the hold he had over her was strongest on the most dangerous, most emotional level.

'All right,' he said at last, his voice as cold and clipped as if it were forced from between lips that had turned to wood, no trace of any emotion in the words at all.

'Very well, milady Katherine, I get the message—loud and clear…'

To Kat's horror he sketched a mocking bow. He even made a pretence—a black, cynical terrible pretence—of tugging at his forelock in a gesture of subservience that she knew was so dreadfully far from what he was feeling—and what she wanted from him—that it turned it upside down, making it the exact opposite of the gesture of deference and turning it into one of stark defiance.

'Oh, don't…' she tried but the words wouldn't leave her tongue so that she heard them only inside her head, the dreadful quiet unbroken by her response.

Heath stepped back, his face turned to carved stone, his eyes just black, black ice.

'I'm sure you will want to take a shower now to erase the taint of a gipsy's touch from your skin. So I'll leave you to do just that.'

'I…' Kat tried but even as she forced the word out he had turned and was striding towards the stairs, holding out his arm so that Isobel could take it as she came slowly down, balancing precariously on the skyscraper heels.

'Are you ready to go?'

'Perfectly. No idea when I'll be back, so expect me when you see me,' Isobel told her sister-in-law with an airy intonation and an even more airy wave. 'You needn't worry—you know I'm in good hands.'

It was exactly whose hands Isobel would be in that worried Kat. But if she begged the younger girl to stay she knew that Isobel would only rebel against her for the sake of it. And besides, what could she say that didn't make it seem that she was indeed as jealous as Heath had accused her of being?

'I'll take very good care of her,' he said now, and the taunting gleam in his eye showed that he recognised the way that his deliberately double-edged comment would hit home to her. 'You need have no worries on that score.'

And while she was still fighting for the clarity of mind to find an answer for him, he swept Isobel out of the door, following her out to the car where he installed her carefully in the front seat before moving round to the other side and sliding into his place beside her.

Could you possibly be jealous, carina?

Heath's words, with that darkly cynical edge on the question, sounded so clearly in her head that if she hadn't been watching him insert his key in the ignition and heard the engine start up she might actually have spun round, looking to see where he had crept up behind her.

I think you are a liar—but a very beautiful one.

Had she been lying? Or had she been telling the deepest, most honest truth? And when? When she had told him that there was no way she was jealous—or when she had been kissing him with all her heart and all her senses? She'd felt that her sister-in-law wasn't safe with Heath, but wasn't the truth the fact that she knew that *she* wasn't safe with him herself? That she was already in so deep that there was no way of escaping, no matter how hard she tried.

She only knew that as she watched the car pull out into the drive and turn away from the house, heading for the gates, the tearing sensation deep inside was far, far worse than it had ever been ten years before when she had learned that he had gone. When she had heard Joe swearing and ranting in a wild black fury that all Heath's jobs had been neglected, the cows not milked, the horses not fed, she had gone to the little rough lean-to and found his bed had not been slept in, his few belongings packed and taken with him, no note or any sort of a message left behind to say where he had gone or whether he ever intended to come back.

She had felt terrible then, lost and lonely and abandoned by the man she had thought of as her friend. But it had been as nothing when compared to the way she was now feeling.

Because this time she knew she had lost him even more than ten years earlier. She had seen that black, bitter look on his face as he had bowed so mockingly before her, heard the viciousness in his tone when he had said, 'Very well, milady Katherine, I get the message—loud and clear...'

It should have been easier, because this time she knew exactly where he was going—and for how long. She knew when he was coming back and in many ways that made it worse because she didn't know how to face him when he did.

CHAPTER SEVEN

A PEAL of thunder broke directly overhead and heavy rain lashed against the car's windscreen as Heath pulled up outside the Grange. The fierce flash of lightning illuminated the main door so brightly that for a moment it was as if someone had turned on a spotlight directly behind them. In the front seat of the powerful vehicle, his passenger, a young boy, stirred and muttered in the shallow sleep he'd fallen into on the difficult journey along the narrow, winding, ill-lit roads across the moors from High Farm.

'Hush.'

Just for a moment he rested a hand on the boy's shoulder, willing him to go back to sleep. Things were bad enough as they were. It would be so much easier if Harry could at least sleep through the rest of the night and let him deal with what had to be done.

With a mutter and a sigh, the boy subsided back under cover of the blanket that he had tucked round him at the start of their journey, leaving Heath free to survey the house before him.

There were no lights on of course, but he had hardly expected anything else. It was almost two in the morning and anyone with any sense would be safely tucked up in bed, with their head under the pillow to block out the noise of the storm. Which was where he should be right now. Alone. No matter what other ideas Isobel Charlton might have had.

A wry smile twisted his mouth at the memory of the way Isobel had reacted when the phone call had come through. She had not been pleased that her lunch date had been cut short so abruptly. Though she'd calmed down easily enough when he'd pointed out that she could still have the table for lunch and invite all her friends—and he would pick up the bill. If only her damn brother-in-law had been as easy to deal with.

Heath rubbed at the bruise on his cheek and cursed Joe Nicholls silently. Just when he had thought that the other man had actually managed to get on the wagon and stop drinking, somehow he'd got hold of a supply of whisky and the result had been one hell of a mess. A mess he'd have been glad to let the fool wallow in if it hadn't been for Harry.

Pushing open the car door, he glanced back at where the boy was curled up on the front seat. Still asleep, thank heaven. But where the devil his fool of a father was now was anyone's guess. Cursing the cold and wet, he pulled his jacket collar up around his ears and hurried to the comparative shelter of the front door. When he pressed the button for the doorbell the sound echoed through the silent house.

'Come on, Kat!'

He muttered the words aloud at the same time that he cursed the fact that he even had to be here, to see her. He would have preferred to leave her alone for the weekend as he had originally planned on. To let her stew for a while. He had thought that they were making progress. That that kiss had brought her close to admitting the desire she felt for him and the sense of dark triumph that had flooded his thoughts had combined with the blaze of hunger in his own body in a dangerously explosive mixture. One that had almost blown up right in his face when she had reacted the way she did.

Even now, just remembering, the blaze of blistering fury was enough to drive away the chill of the night for a short space of time. So hot that he almost expected to see steam rising from his rain-sodden jacket. Kat had melted into his arms, every bit as hungry and willing as he could have dreamed. But then Isobel had come out of her room, and she had reacted like a scalded cat, pulling away and assuming once more the mask of the Lady of the Manor, turning a look of ice on him that made it plain how appalled she was at the thought of being seen kissing him…

Fancy Heath? You have to be joking! Down the years Kat's cool voice, with its lift of mocking laughter, came back to haunt him. *I mean—look at him? No money, no job—no class! The Nicholls family may have fallen on hard times, but we do have some pride. How could anyone want him?'*

'Come *on*!'

He knew that the burn of anger inside him as well as the appalling weather conditions were what drove him to thud his fist against the door, stopping again suddenly at the thought of how she would feel—how anyone would feel—hearing that noise in the middle of the night.

'Katherine!'

He had to raise his voice to shout against the thunder and the roaring wind as it whirled it away again as soon as he had spoken. But at least there was some sign of life inside the house. A light switched on at the top of the stairs, the blurred shape of someone in white he could see through the clouded glass in the big wooden door.

'Who's there?'

'It's Heath! I have to talk to you.'

'Heath?' She sounded horrified. Totally unwelcoming. Which was exactly what he should have expected after the way she had reacted earlier. 'What are you doing here?'

'Katherine, open the door and I'll tell you...'

It suddenly struck him as almost laughably ironic that he was having to ask her to let him in when the truth was that the Grange was actually his property. The documents had been signed only yesterday, with the house and the estate handed over to him in payment for the enormous debts Arthur Charlton had run up. And yet here he was having to ask permission—to plead with her to open the door.

'It's the middle of the night. And it's pouring...'

'I am only too well aware of the time—and the weather conditions! Open the damn door!'

No. That was quite the wrong approach. The way that was guaranteed to have her double bolting the door against him. Probably calling the police for good measure. And right now, the last thing he needed was to get the law involved. Not for his sake but for the sake of her damn brother and the young boy thankfully still asleep in the car. But for how much longer?

'Kat...'

He came close to the door, bent towards the letter box he had pushed open so that she could hear him.

'Let me in, please—you're needed.'

That *please* had Kat freezing on the other side of the door, clutching her white towelling robe around her, pulling it close at the neck as if he could see her clearly.

Had Heath really said *please* and in that tone of voice? That shocking, stunning, almost pleading voice?

Let me in, please—you're needed.

Heath needed her. Just what could have driven him to ask in that way that she let him into her home?

No, she amended painfully, her home no longer. As if she hadn't felt badly enough when Heath had walked out with Isobel on his arm, the car had barely turned out of sight before the phone had rung and Arthur's lawyer had delivered the devastating news that the final, desperate attempt to save something from the wreck of her late husband's life had been unsuccessful. Arthur's creditors had taken everything. There was nothing left.

'Kat...'

...you're needed.

What could Heath possibly need her for? Was he ill? Hurt? Just the thought of it had her reaching for the big heavy bolts at the top and the foot of the door, wrenching the key round in the lock.

The door swung open in a brutal flurry of icy wind and lashing rain, making her shiver convulsively as she peered out into the darkness, trying desperately to see...

'What is it? What's wrong?'

But he had already turned away, moving as soon as he saw the door open. In the light from the hallway she could see his long, straight back, the broad shoulders under the rain-darkened jacket. His black hair tossed wildly in the force of the wind. He was heading back towards the car that was parked slightly askew at the base of the steps. The driver-side door was partly open, the light on, and she could see some sort of dark bundle in the other seat.

'Heath...what is it?'

He ignored her, reaching into the car and picking up... something? Someone?

'It's OK.'

His voice was soothing, calming, but it wasn't directed at her. Instead he spoke down to the bundle he carried. The bundle that stirred against him then settled again as he soothed it once more.

'Open the door, Kat...'

Heath spoke into the wind, the tempest threatening to whirl his words away, but she caught them and stepped back, opening the door wide as he fought his way towards her. Another flash of lightning illuminated the scene wildly as he climbed the steps, strode into the hall, kicking the door to behind him.

'Sitting room...'

He followed right on her heels as she hurried to obey him. It was only when the door had been opened and he had made it into the room, depositing his burden carefully on the sofa and straightening up again, that she managed to pause long enough to look at him properly.

And what she saw brought a shocked gasp to her mouth, her fingers coming up to cover her lips, and her eyes widening above them.

He looked a mess. His jacket, as well as being soaked by the rain, was marked with dark smudges that looked disturbingly like soot, further similar patches on his trousers and his hands. His shirt—the same white shirt he had been wearing when he had arrived earlier that day to collect Isobel—was pulled askew, out of his trousers at his waist and one side of his collar ripped and spotted with blood. There was blood on his mouth from a torn lip and seeping from another cut on his eyebrow. And a heavy, swollen bruise high up on his cheekbone was already darkening to a vivid shade of purple.

Oh, Heath...

And then, looking down at the settee, she saw just what—or rather who—he had placed there.

'Harry? Why have you brought him here? Heath, what happened?'

'What happened?' he asked, flexing tired shoulders and raking both hands through the darkness of his hair, making Kat flinch inside as the movement revealed another bruise on the side of his face. 'Your brother happened—that's what.'

'Joe? What's he done now?'

'He went on a massive bender—downed close to two bottles of whisky in one go. And practically set High Farm and himself on fire. Then when I tried to get into the house to sort things out he went for me...'

A gesture of his long-fingered hand indicated the bruises, the split lip.

'But you were on your way to Leeds.'

'And do you think I would leave the house...' his dark-eyed gaze dropped to the boy, thankfully still asleep, on the settee '...and Harry, unsupervised while I was away? I had someone watching everything that happened. So as soon as trouble started they let me know. And as I hadn't even got halfway down the motorway ...'

'And Isobel?'

Heath had been adjusting his clothing, tucking his shirt back in, fastening buttons, but now he paused, looked her straight in the face.

'She decided she'd rather stay with a friend overnight, once she realised that there was nothing else on offer.'

Nothing else...? Kat didn't know whether relief, shock or plain disbelief was uppermost in her thoughts, only that the combination of all of them made her head spin. But then Heath brushed the back of his hand against the cut on his lip, bringing it away slightly stained with red, and immediately her concern pushed away all other thoughts.

'Let me...'

He swept aside her concern, already turning for the door.

'You take care of Harry. Someone has to find your fool of a brother before he does any more harm.'

'Find him?'

She wished she could do something other than parrot an echo of almost every word he said, but it was still only minutes since she had been dragged from her sleep by his pounding at the door and she was struggling to keep up.

'He's out there somewhere in his car—driving with perhaps a dozen times the legal limit of alcohol in him. I need to find him before he kills someone—or himself. Take care of Harry.'

And then he was gone. Heading back into the driving rain, the ferocious storm that was now so loud overhead that she couldn't hear the sound of his car, only saw the lights sweeping past the windows as he swung the vehicle around and headed off down the drive again.

It was several hours before she saw him again. Several long, sleepless, anxious hours. Harry woke at one point and asked for Heath and then for his father. Unable to find an answer about either of them, she fobbed him off with the vaguest of replies and a hot drink. Then she tucked him up in the bed in the room he always used when visiting and prayed that she would have something to tell him soon.

The storm had growled itself out and was only a low mutter over towards the horizon where dawn was just beginning to turn the sky pink when the sound of Heath's car coming to a halt outside once more dragged her from the weary half-awake state that she'd finally collapsed into. She was up and out of her chair, dashing towards the door and reaching it just as Heath wrenched it open from the other side.

'What's happened? Did you find him?'

She was moving so fast that she ran straight into him, knocking the breath from both their bodies. He took the force of her greeting without a word, arms coming up to clasp round her for a moment.

'Let me sit down, Kat...'

His voice was rough in her ear, so tired that it seemed to be coming apart at the edges.

'It's been one hell of a night.'

Somehow it felt right to take his hand and lead him into the sitting room; to the settee where Harry had been lying a few hours before.

'He's in bed—asleep.' She answered the question Heath's eyes turned on her.

'He woke once but he was worn out.'

Heath nodded silently, his expression closed and shuttered. He looked far worse than when he had arrived the first time, the bruises darker, marking his skin more.

'Joe kept him up very late. He'll probably sleep the clock round.'

And that would be for the best. He didn't have to frame the words; his tone said it for him. As did the weariness in his face and the pale, drawn expression that scored deep lines around his nose and mouth.

'Can I get you a drink?'

She knew only too well what she should really be asking. But she couldn't bring herself to do it. And the look in Heath's eyes warned her that he had no good news to report.

'They gave me a coffee at the police station.'

'Police?'

Was it possible that Joe had just been arrested for drunk driving? Please...

But then, 'Kat...'

Heath simply spoke her name and in spite of having said that he wanted to sit down, he moved towards her and, reaching out, pulled her to him, held her tight in a great bear hug that told her all she needed to know.

He had held her like that when her father had died, she recalled. Crushing her to him so that her face was buried in his shoulder, her cheek against his chest. And just as she had then, now she heard the steady, heavy beat of his heart under the powerful bones, the heat and the scent of his skin reaching her through the fine cotton of his shirt.

It had been on a cold autumn night much like this one and she had been reading, curled up in a corner of the settee while her father dozed in his chair in front of the television. Heath had come to her to tell her it was time to go to bed and she had refused to leave without kissing her father goodnight. As soon as she had looked across the room and seen the way that his head had sunk so low on his chest, his body slumped in the chair, she had known what had happened.

And Heath had been there, just as he was now. There to take her in his arms, to hold her tight when her legs wouldn't support her. To hide her burning eyes against his shoulder, catch her moaning cry of despair against his heart and just wait, saying nothing because there were no words that would help. He had just let her take in the terrible truth, absorb the shock, until she felt ready to face it.

This time was perhaps just that little bit easier because it was not totally unexpected. She had known that Joe was on a downward slope for months. She had seen the same signs as there had been with her husband, and had had little confidence that things would ever be turned around. But she had hoped. And facing the destruction of those hopes was the hardest part of all.

At some point, after a long, brutal silence, Heath must have felt the change in her body, the easing of the terrible tension that had held her tight against him, and recognised the way that she had taken one tiny step towards what she had to face. Then he moved carefully, easing down onto the settee and taking her gently with him. He still held her, her hands in his, his forehead resting against hers, as she drew in a deep, shuddering breath.

'Ask,' he said quietly and suddenly she found that she could.

'What happened?'

'He lost control of the car—the storm would have made things so much worse. He didn't even have the seat belt fastened and he hit the side of a bridge. He would have died almost instantly. In his condition, he probably wouldn't have known a thing.'

'Thank you.'

It was all that she could manage and she felt his grip on her hand tighten, seeming to give her strength and silent support. Somehow, instinctively, he had understood the thing she most needed to know. Hot tears burned at the backs of her eyes but she found they wouldn't fall. That would come later, when the reality of this had sunk in.

'I will have to tell Harry.' Her voice shook terribly on the words.

'I can do that for you if you want.'

'Would you?'

He'd do it for Harry—she knew that in her soul. Something in the boy had reached out to Heath, perhaps reminding him of himself at that same age.

'Of course. You only have to ask. Kat...'

One of the hands that held hers let go and moved upwards, slid under her chin, and lifted her face up towards his. Black, glittering eyes locked with hers and held her, unable to look away.

'I may have hated your brother, but I never wished

him—or your husband—dead. If I could have saved him—found him earlier—I would have done.'

'I know.'

How could she doubt it when the weariness and the look of defeat were stamped on his face, telling her just how he had tried—how disappointed he was that the night had come to this sorry end? She knew from her own restless, miserable wait for his return how terrible it must have been for him when he had the appalling weather conditions to cope with too.

'But I think that both Joe and Arthur were on a path to self-destruction right from the start. Joe was always so bitterly jealous, and his only chance of happiness and living a decent life was with Frances. When she died...'

She shook her head sadly.

'Something of him died too,' Heath put in when she couldn't finish the sentence. 'I can understand that.'

Something flickered in the darkness of his eyes, telling her why he understood, and Kat had to fight to hold back the cry that almost escaped her at the realisation that he understood from *experience*. The thought that he had loved and lost tore at her already weeping heart, making her wince in pain. There was so much in the years they had been apart that she had no way of knowing. So much that had changed him and yet at times, like the moment when he had held her just now, she almost felt she had found the same Heath all over again.

'He got so much worse when he lost Frances. That was why, compared to life at High Farm with Joe's unreliable temper and—even then—his tendency to drink too much, being able to visit the Grange was like escaping into a fairy tale. Where things were calm and beautiful...'

Her voice trailed away and she looked round the room that they were sitting in, recalling how this had been the first room she had ever seen inside the Grange on the night that she and Heath had been caught in the grounds.

'They brought you in here that night...'

It seemed that Heath had picked up on her thoughts. Was she really so transparent or did something give him an extra, unique insight into what was on her mind?

'When the dog bit me?' She nodded slowly, remembering.

They had been out, walking the moors together and were making their way home when she had seen that lights were on in the Grange. She had always wanted to see what the inside of the house was like. The home of the other family that her brother called 'the gentry'. She had just wanted one peep—that was all, she'd begged when Heath had tried to dissuade her. She was a fool, he'd told her. If she went ahead with her plan and got herself into trouble, then she needn't think that he was going to wait around and get her out of it. But she'd ignored his warning and had run across the lawn without thinking, awakening and angering the fierce guard dog so that when she'd fallen it had pounced on her, catching her leg and ankle in its cruel mouth so that she'd fainted from the pain and sheer shock.

'I was lost and frightened. And when I ended up in here with Arthur's mother fussing round me, bathing my leg and making sure I was comfortable, I thought I'd died and gone to heaven.'

'Nothing like the rough and ready conditions at High Farm.'

Again, it was just a statement. But she felt hot colour flood her cheeks at the thought of how much more than 'rough and ready' the conditions he had endured had been.

'No—but...'

She didn't dare to tell him all of it. To let him know

how she had felt almost split in two by the fact that she had been enjoying such comfort and yet there had been a terrible sense of loss because Heath, normally her loyal friend, wasn't there. He'd done just as he'd threatened. Headed back home without a thought for her, leaving her to cope with the fallout from her behaviour. Joe had confirmed that too, when he and Frances had come to visit.

Instead she took the slightly easier—and the safer—way out.

'But what was the nicest part of it was being looked after by Mrs Charlton. She gave me wonderful food—and later a comfortable, clean bed. I'd never been "mothered" in quite that way before. My own mother died when I was only seven so I'd never had any female influence...'

'So that's why you embraced the whole dressing-up-and-painting-your face thing with such enthusiasm.'

'Is that how it seemed? Well, yes, I admit it—I'd never had a chance to do anything like that. And when Mrs Charlton showed me how to do my hair—my make-up—suddenly people weren't laughing at me at school. If Arthur Charlton was interested in me, then...'

No, talking about Arthur had been a mistake. She saw the way his face closed up, eyes becoming cold and flinty. It had been the same when she had come home from the Grange. Things had never been the same after that. Heath had withdrawn from her, become cold and distant. She had turned to Arthur and his friends to fill the gap in her life.

And Arthur had never really wanted her. She had just been a front to conceal his real character, his real inclinations. He must have known even then that her naivety, her longing for acceptance made her the perfect pawn in his cruel, selfish game.

'What happened to us, Heath?' she asked softly, sadly. 'How did we get here from there?'

When he turned another of those cold-eyed looks on her she feared he wasn't going to answer her. But there was something else in his expression that was different. Something that seemed to echo the sense of loss in her own thoughts.

'Life came between us,' he said harshly. 'We grew up. Changed.'

'It was more than that. You drifted away from me—no...' she corrected herself. 'You didn't drift, you took yourself away. You were awkward, hostile—you didn't seem to want to be my friend any more.'

'I sure as hell didn't want to be your *friend*.'

CHAPTER EIGHT

'I SURE as hell didn't want to be your *friend*.'

It was a low, savage-toned growl, one that made her sit up and stare at him in astonishment. The quiet support, the patient listener was gone and in his place was a dark-eyed, harsh-faced man whose change of mood had tightened his jaw, and brought the burn of something dangerous to his eyes.

He had looked like that one night, she remembered, when she had come home from a party, all dressed up, with her hair done in a new sleek style. Mrs Charlton had taken her to the hairdresser and then to the beauty parlour. She had been thrilled with the result, and all her new found friends had been too. At the party there had been boys who had found her attractive, gathering round her in a way she had never known before. She had danced all night, flirted and been flirted with. And she had come home floating on air to be met by Heath with a dark scowl and a vicious sneer marking his face.

'Had fun?' he'd questioned and the cold contempt in his voice had driven her to switch on a similar icy tone of her own.

'The best.' She'd flashed him a wide, over-brilliant smile. 'You wouldn't believe how great it is to spend time with people who know how to have a good time...'

'People with money who know how to spend it,' Heath had growled. 'And you know what they call women who are only with a guy because of the money he'll splash out on them.'

Bitterness had twisted in her heart, the sense of loss all the worse because of the let-down from the high she had been on.

'Lucky?' she'd flashed at him and watched his face tighten even more, his jaw clenching, black fire burning in his eyes.

'Greedy,' he'd tossed back, the acid in the word seeming to strip off a vital protective layer of her skin, leaving her raw and hurting. 'There is another word of course. Much less polite. But I have no doubt that you would go running to your brother to have me thrown out of a job if I used that.'

It was the fact that he thought she'd betray him to Joe that had hurt the worst. She'd lost her temper, lashed out at him. The sound of her hand making contact with the lean plane of his cheek had been appallingly loud in the silence and, shocked at her behaviour, she had only been able to stand and stare as she saw Heath's own hand go up to where the mark of her fingers was swiftly reddening on his skin.

He hadn't uttered another word. Instead he had simply nodded his head just once as if she had confirmed everything he had believed about her. Then he had turned on his heel and walked away.

'Heath...' she had tried but if he'd heard her weak, uncertain voice then he'd ignored it and she hadn't dared to go after him. The fear of another rejection, of facing that arrogant contempt all over again had been more than she could bear.

'I know Joe came between us—and then...'

The words faded from her tongue as he shook his head with slow conviction, rejecting what she was saying.

'It wasn't Joe or even your new-found love of glamour and the high life,' Heath said slowly. 'It was you.'

The way he said it made her head spin. The burn of his eyes made her skin heat until she felt she was in the grip of a burning fever. And from the tension that she could feel in his long, powerful body she could have no doubt of the fight he was having for the rigid control that kept him still in his seat.

'Me?'

What could he mean? How could he mean that?

But then he spoke again.

'You,' he said rawly, and just the sound of his voice took her back to the day when he had first arrived here. When they had been alone in the hall and he had caught her to him and kissed her...

And then he had said, 'If you knew how long I have wanted to do that.'

It had been in just that tone of voice, with the same fierce intensity that left her feeling as if she wanted to duck to dodge the force of his words.

But there was no dodging the impact of what he meant. If she'd wanted to she couldn't have torn her gaze away from the black force of his. And she found that looking away was the last thing she wanted to do. That she was held, mesmerised by what she saw in those eyes. Things she saw for today, for the man he was now, and at the same time recognising the youth he had been. The adolescent, barely more than a boy, who had once been her friend but who, with those few years' advantage of age, and because of the brutal scars of the life he had been forced to live, had grown up more, matured more. He had become a man when she was still lingering in girlhood—still in so many ways a child—so that she hadn't recognised what was growing between them. What he had felt and yet had tried to keep under control.

For her sake.

She had been so stupidly blind.

'Heath…'

She stumbled over his name as if it were suddenly new and very different. As if she had never used it before. And she hadn't. At least not in this way.

'Are you saying…?'

'I wanted you, Kat,' Heath told her jaggedly. 'Wanted you until I was half out of my mind with it. You were in my thoughts every moment of every day, haunted my sleep at night. *Sleep…?*'

His laugh was harsh, cynical, mocking himself cruelly for using the word.

'What sleep? I don't think I slept for days at a time though I tried. God help me, I tried. I worked every hour I could to exhaust myself so that at least I could fall into unconsciousness and forget for a moment. Forget the hunger that was gnawing at me, eating me alive inside. But as soon as I closed my eyes then all hope of sleep would vanish and you would be there again, in my thoughts, in my imaginings.'

Kat was starting to feel as if her mind had become just one huge, million-piece jigsaw, that the night and all that had happened in it had splintered into total disarray. Now, slowly, the pieces were gradually being put back together. But they no longer formed the same image and she didn't think they ever would again.

Heath had wanted her. The words beat a pulse in her veins, pounding at her temples. He had *wanted* her.

'But you never said.'

That earned her a look that was part disbelief, part reproach.

'Of course I never said! For one thing you weren't even legal—it was months to your sixteenth birthday. And for another how would your brother have reacted if he'd known that I—a damn half-breed gipsy—had such lustful thoughts about his sister?'

'You—you never even kissed me.'

'Of course I never kissed you. If I had then I would never have been able to stop. I knew the limits of my control—and you were right at the edge of them. If I'd kissed you it wouldn't have stopped there. And God knows what would have happened if I'd gone so far as to put my dirty hands on you…'

He lifted his hands as he spoke, held them between their two bodies as if to demonstrate that they had once been rough with manual work.

'No, please— No. Don't!'

She caught those hands in hers, held them tight.

'Please don't…' she said more softly.

And she knew deep in her heart that what she was also saying *Please don't* to was the rest of what he had to say. The thoughts he hadn't brought out into the cruel light of day. But she knew that he had to say them. To get them out into the open because they were there, hanging between them, like darkening shadows of memory. The other reasons—the most important reasons—that he had never spoken to her of the way he felt.

And she knew that if he didn't say them, then she would have to do so for him.

'Is that it?' she asked nervously.

'It's enough, isn't it?'

'No, it's not enough—because even if I said "don't" the reality is that I need it all. I need the truth. Please, Heath, let's have the truth between us. Surely now, at last, we can do that.'

'What do you want me to say?'

'It was because of me, wasn't it? Because of the way that I changed? The time I spent with Arthur—here in the Grange. The different things I wanted from life.'

His eyes had dropped to their linked hands and she felt the barriers come up between them again.

'You sure as hell didn't make it easy to get close to you.'

'I'm amazed that you stayed at all. After the way that Joe behaved. And then when Arthur joined in. That you didn't just turn and walk away so much earlier.'

Heath's reaction to her words startled her. It was as if she had caught him on the raw somehow, sticking a sharp point into him so that he got to his feet in a rush, pacing around the room like a restless, caged hunting cat.

What had she said? How had she got to him so strongly?

'Why—why didn't you go?'

The flashing sidelong glance from those brilliant dark eyes told her that she should not need an answer. That she should be able to find one for herself. But she needed him to say it. Her mind felt as if it were being torn in two, not knowing whether she longed to hear him say what was in her thoughts or dreaded that that was what was coming.

'Heath—please.'

At last he stopped his restless pacing. He stood in the middle of the room and faced her, his strong body taut, his face a mask of control.

'I stayed for you.'

'For me...'

Her echoing of his words was just a sigh. And it seemed that her heart was alternately dancing at the thought that he had felt that way and clenching in panic at the implications of that stark statement. Had he really put up with so much ill-treatment from her brother—the scorn and mockery that Arthur too had indulged in—*for her*?

'I thought that you were too young, too blind, to realise what your brother had in mind.'

Did he mean what she thought? The grim look on his face frightened her, telling her that whatever she suspected it was probably only scraping the surface.

'High Farm needed money. Charlton had plenty—or so it seemed. A wedding between the two of you would be just what he wanted. And Charlton wasn't against the idea.'

'They had it planned all along? Even then?'

New pieces of the jigsaw puzzle were falling into place. Ones that made everything appear in a very different focus, making her realise how things had never been quite the way they had seemed.

Joe had encouraged her visits to the Grange. He had found money—from heaven knew where—so that she could buy the clothes that Mrs Charlton had suggested, go to the clubs that Arthur and his friends frequented. And all the time Heath had seemed to move further and further away from her.

But wasn't the truth that she had moved further away from him?

And it had been around that time that her brother had become more and more vindictive towards Heath, making him work inhumanly long hours, keeping him out of the house. If she was honest, some of that had been a relief to her rather than have to face his dark disapproval every time she went out or came home late.

How many times had she asked herself why he didn't just tell her brother to go to hell and walk out?

I stayed for you.

She had been too blind and foolish to see what he was

doing. She hadn't been able to read his dark, complex character. And she had been flattered by Arthur's apparently charming attentions. She had learned her mistake there very painfully.

'About Arthur—'

She owed Heath this, even if it shamed her to admit just how wrong she had been.

'I thought I knew him, but in the end I found he was not the man I believed. Like Joe, he was always gambling, always losing more money than he could ever afford. When he died, the number of creditors who came out of the woodwork was scary. It seemed that everyone wanted something—more money than I had ever dreamed anyone could spend in a lifetime.'

Heath didn't look surprised—or even shocked. And the total calmness of his reception of her confessions was such a relief after months of living with the shocked faces, the whispering behind hands, the twitching of window curtains, the dread of everything coming out.

'But it was worse than that—there were drugs. I was so naïve—I didn't guess any of that. He was hooked on heroin—and he spent so much of his time in seedy clubs where he could feed his habit, drink his head off...'

She knew she was gabbling, that the words were just pouring out of her, but it was as if someone had just ripped off the gag that had been over her mouth ever since she had discovered the truth about her marriage. And that had been in the very first week of her honeymoon. She had never been able to share this with anyone before, and she found that Heath's silence was the perfect encouragement to go on.

'Why did you marry him?' It was just a question, no reproach, no recrimination.

'I made the biggest mistake of my life.'

It was only as she spoke the words that the stab of something raw threatened her with the realisation of just how much of a mistake she had made. What she had lost by ever choosing Arthur over Heath.

'I—I thought that Arthur, with his ready smile, his easy laugh, was the charmer he had at first appeared to be. And that life at the Grange was that dream come true. But my first instinct when I came round in this room was to call for you because I felt so lost and afraid. The Charltons had soon made me feel more relaxed and cared for. But I should have listened to those instincts. Because that time that I first ended up here, you didn't just leave me, did you?'

She didn't need the shake of his dark head to confirm her suspicions.

'They threw me out,' he stated flatly.

'They were trying to split us up even then. And I let them.'

'You only had to ask.'

'I was too proud. Too stupid. You said you'd leave me and…'

Impulsively she moved forward, put a hand on his arm, curled her fingers around the hard warm strength of muscle and bone. Suddenly it seemed that there was only this that she could hold onto in a world that had splintered crazily around her. From that moment when, hurt and lost, she had swallowed Joe and Arthur's version of the truth she had let them get into her mind, and she had seen Heath's behaviour through the distorting mirror of their lies and deceit. Because of that she'd lost the best friend she'd ever had.

'Heath, I'm sorry. So sorry. I wish I could go back and change how it was.'

'We can't change the past,' he said soberly. 'But we can

stop repeating it. We can get off this treadmill and start again.'

'Can we? Can we really start again?'

She didn't care if her voice revealed how much that would mean to her. She *wanted* it to show him how she felt.

'We can try.'

A hand on his arm was not enough. She wanted to be closer, to touch him—hold him...

She wanted to kiss him. Surely a kiss was the way to seal this? At least to hold out the promise of rebuilding the trust there had once been.

'I'd love that...'

She stood on tiptoe as she spoke, lifting her face to press a kiss on the lean plane of his cheek. She didn't dare to risk trying for his lips. It would shatter her if he resisted or, worse, rejected the caress, closing his mouth against it, so that it would be like kissing a carved wooden statue, not a living breathing human being. The man she ...

Shock stopped her breath, made her heart freeze just for a moment. She couldn't complete the thought, not rationally, her brain whirling at the impact of the word that was hovering just out of reach.

But the taste of his skin was still on her lips, and the realisation was like an explosion in her thoughts.

Love. That was the word she wanted.

Heath was the man she *loved*.

'Kat...'

The sound of his voice started her pulse up again. She could breathe and move and the room was the same, the hazy light of the dawn was the same. But something had changed so deeply and so fundamentally that she knew she could never go back.

'I'd love that,' she repeated because she didn't dare to say the words that were really on the tip of her tongue.

As she leaned in to kiss him again this time he gave a muttered curse. Something in the language he was used to speaking. Something so far from the Yorkshire voices she heard all around her every day that it added to the sense of unreality. This time he turned his head so that their mouths met and fused. And nothing was the same. How could it ever be like anything she had ever known? She felt as if she had never been kissed in her life before. And she hadn't—at least not like this.

A sound like the buzzing of thousands of crazy bees sounded inside her head, wild and whirling, drowning out thought, leaving only room for response. Her mouth opened under his, inviting the intimate invasion of his tongue, and her bones seemed to melt so that she swayed against him, needing the strength of his body to lean on, the muscles in the arms that had come round her to hold her up. She had lost herself and knew only him, the heat of his skin, the scent of his body, the taste of his mouth. He was everywhere, surrounding her, supporting her, enclosing her, and the heavy pulse of her blood seemed to pool at the juncture of her thighs, throbbing wildly under the impact of the need that was raging through her.

'*Querida, anja...*'

Heath's muttered response was a wild litany of Portuguese against her lips, each word punctuated by another demanding kiss.

She wasn't sure whether it was the impact of those kisses or the pressure of his body on her but somehow they were walking backwards, stumbling, moving blind, until they ended up with her back against the wall, Heath's arms on either side of her, his body crushing hers, so that the full swollen evidence of his arousal was hot against her stomach, his hips cradling hers.

The front of the white towelling robe that she had thrown on to hurry down and answer the door, kept on throughout the long anxious night, was wrenched apart, tugged part way down her arms, imprisoning them at her sides and revealing the pale blue cotton nightdress she wore underneath. Heath's hot, hungry mouth left her lips and kissed its way down the side of her jaw, along the line of her throat, moving lower to the deep vee neck that revealed just the start of the curves of her breasts.

'Oh, Heath!'

His name was a sigh of longing, of yearning and her body arched against him, only the wall at her shoulders offering any support. Her breasts felt full and heavy, her nipples peaking against the fine cotton, her hips writhing against his, forcing a harsh, abandoned groan from his mouth. A groan that was echoed, wilder and more urgent, when that tormenting mouth closed over one swollen peak of her breast, swirling his tongue over the distended bud and drawing on it through the dampened material, making her feel that she would faint with the stinging blend of aching hunger and mind-blowing delight.

'Heath...'

She needed more. She needed to touch him, feel his skin, get closer still. In the struggle, to free her trapped arms, the white robe was shrugged off completely, slipping down to pool on the floor at her feet, ignored as she reached for him, tugging at the fastenings on his shirt, wrenching them open with such haste, such a total lack of finesse that she heard a button snap off and go flying into the room, landing somewhere unseen and unnoticed. Kat's own breath hissed in through her teeth as at last her fingertips felt the burning heat of his flesh, the smooth ridges of muscles, her hands stroking, teasing, tangling in the soft down of his body hair.

Heath muttered something again, something she could barely hear through the throb of her pulse at her temples. The same racing pulse that pounded in the vulnerable spot at the base of her throat, pushed into overdrive by the hot pressure of his mouth against it, the moist caress of his tongue.

'I want you.'

She barely recognised the hoarse and hungry voice as her own, the words breaking, cracking in the middle as she gasped for the breath that seemed to have locked inside her throat.

'Want you...'

Her knees were giving way; she was sinking down onto the floor onto the cushion of the tumbled robe. But with her hands clutching at him, fingers clenched around his arms, she brought Heath down with her, drawing him closer and closer until his long hard body was half kneeling, half lying across her. Her nightdress had rucked up around her waist, exposing the pallor of her thighs and the dark shadow of hair between her legs. Against her exposed skin, the heated pressure of his weight was a glorious imprisonment, a promise of the fulfilment that she craved so much that she was trembling all over with the hunger that had her in its grip.

'It's been a terrible, terrible night but this...'

She was reaching up to hook her arm around his neck, draw his face down to her for one more yearning kiss when she realised that something had changed. That the mood was suddenly wrong, suddenly so far from the heated passion of just moments before that the unexpected cooling of her senses, the draught of chilling air that swept over her made her shiver in the ice of shock and too sudden a withdrawal.

'Heath?' She had to struggle to open her eyelids to look up at him through blurred vision. 'What?'

'*Não!*' he said roughly, vehemently. '*Não!*' And then as if there might be any doubt that he meant what the word sounded like, he repeated in forceful English, 'No way!'

If he had slapped her hard in the face it couldn't have left her feeling any more shocked and disorientated. She couldn't find any words, or any thought of the right way to react. She felt she should sit up, move away, at least gather herself together so as to cope, but she lacked the strength, the ability to do so. It was only the floor at her back that gave her any support and even that felt as if it were actually swaying, listing up and down like the floor on some ship on an unsettled sea until she felt quite nauseous with it.

'What—Heath...?' was all she could manage and she wasn't even sure whether he heard that or not as his long body jack-knifed up and away from her, getting to his feet to tower above her, his face dark and shuttered against her.

'I said no,' he declared, cold, hard and totally unyielding. 'This isn't going to happen. Not tonight. Not like this.'

'But...'

Not like this...not like this... The words were a bitter refrain inside her head. And she didn't know whether it was Heath's words or her own memories that put them there. Not like this. She couldn't bear it if Heath, like Arthur, turned away from her—rejected her as a woman. But surely he had *wanted* her—it had felt so very different from any time she had been with Arthur. Heath had been an ardent, passionate force. He had more than met her halfway. He had been the one instigating this. But something she had said or done...

At last she found she could sit up, pushing her hands against the floor to try to raise herself to her feet. But it seemed that she'd exhausted all the strength she had and already he was moving away from her, hands going rather wildly to smooth the hair she had ruffled back into place, pushing down his shirt, shoving it any way into the waist of his jeans, careless of the fact that it was still unfastened over his chest.

'I said no.' It came from between gritted teeth as if it was the only sound he trusted himself to make. 'And I meant no.'

Just what had happened? Where had things gone so wrong so suddenly? He had been with her every inch of the way—or so she'd thought. And then suddenly—as if someone had unexpectedly thrown a switch—nothing! It had all just stopped—gone—evaporated—as if the blazing passion she had sensed between them had never existed.

Or had she got it all wrong from the start? Face it, Kat, she told herself, you have little enough experience on which to base these things. Marriage to a man who didn't know how to arouse a woman, who quite frankly wasn't even interested. A man who, she knew now, had never stirred her senses in the way that the big, dark, dangerous man before her managed to do with just a look, a smile—a kiss. So wasn't it possible that she had lost all trace of understanding, of self-preservation in the inferno of need that he had sparked off inside her, leaving her at the mercy of her newly awakened libido that was clamouring for the heated satisfaction it had never known but now sensed was just about within touching distance if only…?

And it was that *if only* that had got things so wrong. *If only* Heath had been as hotly involved as she had too. *If only* he had wanted her as much as he had said he wanted her when he had been a lonely adolescent and she an immature and naïve girl who hadn't understood these things. She understood them now; understood them far too well. But what she feared, and what made her heart clench and twist in sudden panic, was that she had only come to this discovery far, far too late.

All that time in the past he had wanted her and she hadn't known it. Now she wanted him so desperately but it seemed that he no longer felt the same way about her.

And the worst part of all, that sharpened the knife that was already twisting in her soul, was the realisation that she loved him. She knew now what loving someone, really loving them so deeply that you felt even your souls were the same, truly felt like and because of that she was forced to recognise that she had always, always loved him. Even when she had thought that he was not the one for her, even when she had been so blinded, seduced by Arthur and his family, the Grange, the whole package, even then, deep down, so deep down that she hadn't been able to find it, she had loved him.

That was why it had hurt so terribly when he had walked away.

But Heath had walked away because he would not betray her. He had known that his feelings then were too strong, too fierce, for the child she was. He had protected that girl, stayed in an appalling situation, endured her brother's cruelty, his insults, because of her and he had shown his care for her, by walking away too.

Joe... Oh, Joe!

The memory hit hard, devastating her with the reminder of how this evening had begun. The terrible events that had brought her and Heath together. Her hand went to her mouth to hold back the sob of pain. Joe had had his faults—so many faults and more, it seemed, than she had ever truly understood. But he had been her brother.

Not like this...

Something she had said or done.

Now, as her mind cleared, as something of the agony of rejection lessened, she could hear herself saying, *It's been a terrible, terrible night but this...*

Was that it? Was it possible that even now Heath was still protecting her, defending her—against herself? He knew what the night had taken from her, how lost and bereft it had left her, how vulnerable...and so he would not take advantage of it. Not even when it was the thing she most wanted in all the world.

Not like this...

But if not like this then when? If ever?

She didn't dare to ask. Couldn't risk the chance that right here and now he might say *never*. And she couldn't argue with him. Just like that time in the past, when Joe had thrown him out of the house and she had had to let it happen because she couldn't fight Heath himself, she knew she could never change his mind over this.

'I'll come back later if you want me to talk to Harry.' Heath had reached for his jacket and was shrugging himself into it. 'Anything I can do.'

'Thank you.'

Feeling terribly vulnerable and horribly exposed sitting there in her crumpled nightdress, her bare legs stretched out in front of her, Kat scrambled to her feet.

'Heath...'

Something in the way he looked at her made her reach down and snatch up the white towelling robe, meaning to scramble into it to cover herself. But she found that her hands were shaking and it was all she could do to hold it up in front of her, clutching it to her. The gesture pressed the fine cotton of her nightgown, still damp from his mouth, against her sensitised breasts, sending the stinging burn of arousal coursing through her still trembling body so that for a moment she totally forgot what she had been about to say.

'Yes?' he prompted harshly when she hesitated. 'What did you want?'

'Want? Oh—I—I just wanted to ask—'

Faced with that cold-eyed stare, she knew that if it hadn't been so very important to her she wouldn't be able to find the strength to get it out. The warm, passionate, sensual Heath who had been in her arms just moments before had vanished, leaving in his place a stranger carved from black ice. A man she didn't know how to reach.

'Will you—will you come to the funeral—please?'

Now what had she done to make him still like that? What had she said that would make his face close up so completely?

And what was it that had flickered deep in his eyes and then went out again as if someone had touched a switch? But when that look had faded it left everything in his face somehow different like a glass of water that had had a single drop of dark concentrate blended through it.

Of course, she told herself, mentally kicking herself hard. Idiot! You complete, total idiot! She had asked the impossible, letting her own needs blind her to how he must actually be thinking. Why would he even want to think about attending the funeral of the man he had hated so much?

I'm sorry... But just as she opened her mouth to say the word, retract her request, Heath nodded just once, sharply, abruptly.

'Yes,' he said at last. 'If you want me, I'll be there.'

CHAPTER NINE

THE door had finally closed on the last person who had called to pay their respects at the Grange and from the kitchen Heath heard Kat sigh and stretch wearily, muttering a heartfelt, 'At last!' as she finally relaxed in the almost empty house.

'All gone?'

'All gone,' she agreed. 'Thank the Lord! I know people only want to be kind—to express their sympathies—but it's been nearly two weeks now and still they're coming.'

'They're concerned about you.'

'I know—and I'm grateful, really I am.' Kat appeared in the doorway, rubbing her hands over her eyes. 'But I'm so tired and talking to people every day just keeps bringing it home to me. You didn't have to do that!' she added, looking round the kitchen.

'What? Clear away a few cups?' Heath shrugged off her comment. 'Load the dishwasher? It's hardly going to exhaust me.'

'No, but—well, I didn't expect...'

'I am quite housetrained. And remember, I once used to actually do the washing up—with hot water in the sink and everything.'

That brought a brief smile to her wan, tired face.

'So you did—but not here of course. Up at High Farm

maybe. Remember how we always used to argue over who washed and who dried?'

'And you used to always insist that I should wash because my nails had dirt in them after I'd been grooming the horses or mucking out their stalls.'

'You used to spend every hour you could out in the stables.' Slowly, Kat shook her head, sending the sleek ponytail in which she had fastened her dark hair flying. 'There are no horses up at High Farm now—haven't been any for a long time.'

A sudden thought obviously struck her and she straightened up from where she had been leaning against the doorframe.

'Do you still ride? Do you have any horses out in Brazil?'

'Some.'

Heath slammed the door of the dishwasher shut with rather too much force and switched it on. For a moment the rush of water into the machine was the only sound in the room as his thoughts went to be the huge estate he owned in Brazil, the sleek, beautiful thoroughbreds that were in the fields behind the house. Horses that had fabulous bloodlines but had never meant as much to him as the sturdy little nag that Mr Nicholls had let him ride. A pony that Joe had once taken from him when his own mount had gone lame. The house and the land surrounding it was more than he had ever dreamed of owning but somehow had never become a home.

Not like—impossibly—the Grange had actually felt over the past two weeks. At first he had just acknowledged the lift of his spirits when he turned into the drive that led to the big house, that, in spite of the recent bereavement, still held a warmth and a welcome that had been missing in his existence for years. All his life, to be honest. Except for that one brief spell when Kat's father had taken him in and he had felt that at last he might have found somewhere where he belonged.

'You're tired...' He pulled out a chair, gestured towards it. 'Come and sit down and I'll make you a drink.'

'Not more tea!' Kat's laugh was rough-edged but still held genuine amusement. 'I feel as if I'm awash with the stuff. I've done little else but drink tea ever since...'

The weak smile vanished, and he saw the sheen of tears film her eyes.

'You've managed brilliantly.'

'Someone had to.'

She moved across the room but ignored the chair he had pulled out as she looked up into his face. The shadows under her blue eyes gave them a bruised look in her pale face and he suspected that, like him, she hadn't slept well for the two weeks since Joe's accident.

'And you've been such a help. I do wish you'd accept my invitation and come and stay here rather than camping out at High Farm.'

'And what would the neighbours think?'

He tried to keep his tone light when the truth was that her closeness was creating torture in his body as he fought with the hungry libido that surfaced every time he saw her. A hunger that made it far easier to stay in discomfort at High Farm rather than accept the invitation Kat had made when she had seen the mess that Joe had created on his last day of drunken debauchery.

If she only knew what sort of a living hell it would be to be with her here in her home, see her every day, know she was in the shower or, worse, in her bed—the bed she had once shared with her husband. It was bad enough trying to sleep when he was miles away. As he lay awake at night his last thoughts before sleep were of her, and then, when he finally managed to drift into a restless and un-settled doze, she was there in his dreams. Tempting, erotic dreams that had plagued him hard until he had woken drenched in sweat and with his heart racing.

It was a terrible, bitter irony that he had told himself he was going to wait until she came to him, that she was going to have to ask him to make love to her—and yet when she had done just that then he had had to turn away, declare that this was not going to happen. Because how could he believe what she had said that night? How could he accept that she knew what she was doing, that she was even thinking straight?

He had just told her that her brother was dead, and she had turned to him in a moment of terrible loss and dark despair. How could he trust that? And how could he take advantage of it when in the cold light of day she would come back to herself and consider her impulsive decision to be the very worst mistake of her life? He had endured her rejection once in his life and had barely survived it. He wasn't at all sure that he could deal with it all over again. And whatever he might have believed he wanted when he had first arrived in Hawden, the one thing he knew now was that he most definitely could not put Kat through the misery of regretting what she had done. She had enough on her plate.

And so he had kept his distance though it almost killed him to do so.

'Do you know, I don't think I care,' Kat said, her voice lifting for the first time in too long. 'And anyway…'

He thought he knew what made her voice trail off. What made her white teeth dig into the softness of her bottom lip. The way she looked around her, her clouded gaze tak-ing in the kitchen, the rest of the house, the garden beyond the window brought the words he could use to soothe the anxiety stinging on his tongue.

'Let them think what they like,' she finished. 'It's none of their business.'

Heath checked his watch. He had planned to wait until everything was signed and sealed, but surely it was best not to delay any longer. Perhaps if they shared a drink they could talk...

'So if you don't want tea, is almost seven-thirty too early for a glass of wine?'

'I'd like that.'

She fetched glasses and put them on the table, settled into the chair he had pulled out while he eased the cork from the neck of the bottle.

'Did Harry ring?'

The boy was staying with a school friend, sleeping over at his home. It helped to distract him, to take his mind off what had happened and to divert his thoughts from the emptiness in the house where his father had once been. His presence in the Grange had helped Heath too. He and Harry had gone for long walks, swum in the indoor pool, or kicked a ball about on the lawn.

Kat nodded.

'He said that he and Mark are going to watch a DVD tonight. Some thriller that he was sure I wouldn't approve of, but I think he can be indulged a little right now. He asked where you were—I think he's developing quite a dose of hero worship where you're concerned.'

Heath made a non-committal sound that might have been agreement, his attention fixed surprisingly closely on the glass he was filling with rich red wine.

Harry wasn't the only one who had a bad case of hero worship for Heath, Kat reflected. In the past days, he had become a welcome fixture in her life and quite frankly she didn't really know how she would have coped without him. From the very start, with Harry going into shock and refusing to speak to anyone, Heath had been the only one who could get through to him. Perhaps it was because he knew how it felt to have life hit you in the face at a very early age, or perhaps because he shared the young boy's interest in horses and football, but the two of them had formed a quiet friendship that had got Harry through some terrible moments. Heath had also dealt with Isobel's hysterics when she had arrived home and found the house in mourning and preparations being made for Joe's funeral.

The funeral. Kat reached for the nearest glass of wine and took a sip as memories swamped her. She didn't know how she would have got through that without Heath at her back. There to deal with problems that arose, to turn to when difficult decisions needed to be made, to support her when things became just too much to take. The last weeks had been like going back to the time when she had lived in peace and security in High Farm with Heath at her side. But she knew he couldn't be here for ever. Some time soon he would leave, go back to the world he had built for himself in another continent and she would have to face life without him. She'd done it once before but this time would be so much worse. Then she had just been a child, losing a childhood friend. Now she would be losing the man she loved.

Heath pulled out a chair for himself and sat opposite her at the kitchen table, picking up his own glass. Casually dressed in a navy long-sleeved tee shirt and denim jeans, he was devastating up this close. The late day's growth of beard on his strong jaw together with the green glow of the earring in his lobe gave him back the piratical look that had hit her so hard on the day he had first walked back into this house. A look that had been hidden underneath the sombre, dignified man at the funeral or the much younger looking, relaxed and easy-going Heath who had spent so much time with Harry.

The bruising on his face had faded, the split lip healed, but she still winced at the thought that her brother had done that to him, once again using force and violence when his temper had boiled over. She'd been appalled too by the state High Farm had been in when she'd gone up there before the funeral. She'd asked Heath to come and stay in the Grange. It had been the least she could do

'I hate to think of you going back to High Farm tonight,' she said now, remembering.

'It isn't as bad as it was.' Heath's black eyes met her concerned blue ones over the top of his glass. 'I got some men in to start work on the worst problems. They're making great progress.'

It was polite and careful, as he had been ever since the night she had practically thrown herself at him, but it was still a rejection. But then what had she expected? Had she hoped that he would change his mind? That perhaps one night he would forget the way he had declared 'this isn't going to happen'? Who was she kidding?

And yet... That dark, desperate dawn she would have sworn that he was every bit as aroused, as hotly hungry as she had been.

'It will be amazing to see the place restored to something of its former glory.' She aimed for casual, even came close to hitting it. 'How long do you think that will take?'

'A few weeks—a month maybe.'

'What will you do with the place when it's all done up?'

'I have plans.'

Plans that he didn't intend to share with her, his tone said, and she took another unwary mouthful of wine in an attempt to conceal the twisting stab of pain at the way his carefully guarded façade meant that every attempt she made to get closer simply bounced off his armoured defences.

In a few weeks then he would probably be gone, heading back to the wealthy life he had built for himself away from here. He had had scores to settle, he had said, and they must be behind him now.

Soon she would be on her own again, and she would have to try to start looking to the future. But what sort of a future that might be she had no idea. There would be nothing left of the old life, that was sure.

If there was one relief it was that at least the company that wanted to take over the Grange—the company that now *owned* the Grange—had stepped back, and given her some space. Unexpectedly, they had sent a message to her lawyer offering their sympathy on her loss and offering her some weeks' grace while she sorted things out on a personal level. She had never expected such generosity, but the time of armistice couldn't last for ever. The house was no longer hers. Soon she would have to pack up the few things that still belonged to her and were not being taken in payment of Arthur's monstrous debts—and she would have to leave.

And it would be so much worse because this was the only home that Harry had now.

Perhaps Heath would be able to help. Not financially, of course. She couldn't ask that of him but perhaps he could give her some advice, suggest a way forward. She had opened her mouth to ask but then a rush of memory made her close it again. She had no idea what was going through Heath's mind these days and knew only that there was some sort of peace between them. She didn't want to risk opening old wounds or, worse, driving him to walk out again.

The thought of how she would feel if that happened made her nerves twist in sudden panic so that her hand jerked as she lifted the glass to her lips again, some of the wine missing her mouth and trickling down towards her chin.

'Careful…'

Heath moved quickly, leaning forward to press a couple of fingers against her mouth so as to stop the rich red liquid before it dropped any further, spilled onto her white shirt. He caught the wine, letting it run onto his fingers, then froze, deep, impenetrable black eyes locking with hers and holding still.

'Thanks…'

At least that was what Kat meant to say, but her voice cracked, failed her halfway through the word so that all that came out was *Thaa*… But that was enough to bring her tongue to her lips, to make it brush against those warm hard fingers, taste the faintly salty tang of his skin that was mixed with the intense flavour of the wine.

And having tasted it once she couldn't turn away. She felt her heart jolt hard in her chest, and couldn't stop herself from letting her tongue slip out again, touch, taste— and this time she let it slide over his fingers, slicking a trail of temptation all the way along them.

She heard his breath hiss in sharply, could tell from his total stillness the effect the tiny caress had had on him, and her breath seemed to tie itself in a knot in her throat. She wanted to speak, to say his name, but her voice had deserted her and still his hand hadn't moved away from her face. Her mouth was dry and when she sent her tongue out again to moisten her lips she caught another intensely personal taste of Heath's skin.

'Kat…'

Heath's voice sounded rough and hoarse and she knew

that she would sound exactly the same if she tried to speak. And suddenly she had a long-ago memory of a time when she had heard just that raw note in his use of her name and had been too naïve to interpret it right.

She knew exactly what it meant this time.

'I am going to kiss you. And if that is not what you want, then…'

'That's exactly what I want.'

And to prove it, she leaned forward, mouth slightly open, eyes fixed on his.

Their breath merged in the seconds before their mouths touched and for Kat that was a moment that was intimate enough for her almost to want to pause and stay just the way they were. To enjoy the anticipation with the scent of his skin in her nostrils, the warmth of his breathing on her face…

Almost. Because even as she closed her eyes to appreciate the sensations that rippled through her Heath's mouth touched hers in a kiss that gave, tempted, seduced all in one instant. And in that instant suddenly anticipation was very definitely no longer enough.

The taste of him was all that she wanted; but she also wanted more. The feel of his mouth on hers was the promise of fulfilment; but she wanted more than a promise. The closeness of his long, strong frame to hers was nothing like enough. She remembered the hot, heavy weight of him on top of her before, and she wanted that all over again.

She wasn't sure which one of them moved first. Only knew that they both moved and that from sitting at the table, with the scrubbed pine surface between them, they were suddenly in each other's arms, with nothing between them but the clothes that did little to conceal or even mask the heat and hunger for skin on skin that burned them up.

Heath's mouth on hers was as hungry as her own, seeking, yearning, taking. The intimate dance of their tongues silently invited and provoked, quickening their breathing, making their heartbeats pound.

'*Querida...namorada,*' Heath muttered thickly in the one moment that he snatched his lips away to drag in a rough, much-needed breath. But even the few seconds taken to say the words was too long, making Kat feel starved of pleasure, ravenous for more, so that she clamped her arms up around his neck, dragged his head back down towards hers, and took for herself the kisses she so desperately needed.

Another couple of thundering heartbeats took them to a place where that was no longer enough and their arms bumped and clashed, hands tangling together, coming between their bodies as each of them tried to snatch at the other's clothing, find fastenings, openings, any way at all to get rid of the restrictions on their closeness, open them up to more intimacy.

Heath was pushing her back against the table, her hips bumping against the wooden top. Her back was arched almost to the point where she was lying back on it and she let loose a shaken laugh as she heard the heavy legs scrape against the tiled floor as it was pushed back under their combined weight.

One of his hands was in her hair, the loose ponytail long since pulled completely free so that his long fingers could twist in the slippery strands, tangling so tight so that he could hold her just where he wanted her for the pressure of his kiss to take her mouth completely, forcing it wide open under his to allow his probing tongue the total access that he sought. The fingers on the other hand had found the buttons down the front of her blouse, ripping them open with blatant lack of concern for any damage they might have done to the fine material. Not that Kat gave a damn either, that wondering, encouraging laughter bubbling up in her throat once again. But in the moment that his hand touched her skin, hot fingers roughly pushing her slip aside, snapping the delicate straps as he sought the swell of her breast. Then all thought of laughter was blasted from her mind in a mind-blowing explosion of sensation that left her grateful for the support of the table at her back, her legs shaking too much to hold her upright without it.

But the truth was that, even with it, she was not going to be able to stay upright for a moment longer. The heat that pulsed between her legs seemed to have taken all of the strength from her limbs and it was only by clutching onto Heath's powerful frame that she stopped herself from sliding limply onto the floor, slipping into a molten pool of arousal right at his feet.

'How are we going to do this?' she muttered in Heath's ear, sliding her tongue around the shape of it, closing her teeth over the emerald stud and biting down around its edges and drawing a heated, yearning groan from him. 'Where?'

Because there was no longer any doubt that they were going to do this. She would die if they didn't. If he stopped now...

But Heath had obviously no intention of stopping and, only pausing to look deep into her eyes, planted another fierce kiss on her mouth, before he swung her up into his arms, hands hot against her legs, and turned towards the door.

'Upstairs,' he muttered, voice raw, eyes intent, as he headed towards the wide staircase, his long strides already taking them partway along their journey before the word was completed.

They were already halfway up the wide, curving staircase when his progress slowed, halted, and he looked down at her suddenly, a new and shockingly vulnerable expression in the darkness of his eyes. A vulnerability blended with ruthless determination and a stunning resolution.

'*Your* room,' he said thickly, a world of meaning behind the words. 'Not...'

He didn't need to finish the sentence, she understood immediately just what he meant.

Her room. *Her* bed.

Not the bed she had once shared with Arthur in this house as husband and wife.

'*My* room,' she echoed, knowing he had never needed to ask. There was no way she would have wanted her first time with Heath to be in the matrimonial bed she had once shared with the man he had hated.

Her *first* time.

The words seemed to slap against her head like a blow, sending her thoughts spinning at the thought of what she had forgotten. What Heath's kisses, his touch, had made her forget. And there was no way she could let that stay unmentioned for a moment longer. She didn't know if it would change things. She prayed it wouldn't alter a thing. But she still had to tell him.

So when Heath kicked open the door to the room she had indicated—the room she had moved into when her disaster of a marriage had become too much to bear, long before Arthur's sordid and wretched death—and took her over to the bed, she let herself be tumbled onto the downy coverings, but at the same time she reached up and held him, framing his face between her hands.

'Heath...' she said softly, but with a firmness that reached him even through the blaze of lust that she could see was glazing his eyes, putting a streak of heat across

the wide, carved cheekbones. 'There is something you
need to know.'

'Kat…'

It was a groan of protest but all the same he stilled, long
body tense above her and she saw the brutal struggle he
had to control himself. She knew how he felt; the same
hunger was burning through her, making this so hard to
do. But this had to be said.

'I know—but—Heath… The bed—my bed…'

She was stumbling over her words, tying herself up in
knots and making her tongue feel as if it were tangled in
her mouth. Snatching in a deep, courage-giving breath,
she brought it out in a rush.

'You have *no* memories of Arthur to worry about. We
never—in this bed or in any other. Oh, hell, what I'm trying to say is that I've never done this before.'

'You…'

For a moment Heath looked as if he had been slapped
hard in the face. The powerful body froze. His head went
back sharply and his eyes narrowed in sharp assessment.

'You've never…'

'Never,' Kat assured him on a whisper. *'Never.'*

He was too still, too silent, and suddenly fear was a
cold, creeping sensation along her nerves. Had she said
too much?

'Too much?'

It was only when Heath echoed her words that she realised to her horror that she had spoken them out loud.
Already her body was stinging in the aftermath of the
withdrawal from the erotic sensations that had flooded it
so that she moved restlessly on the bed.

'Never, *querida*. You do not know what a gift you have
given me.'

Bending his head again, he took her lips in a kiss that swept away all doubt, all hesitation, all fear.

'You are mine,' he muttered against her lips. 'Only mine. As you should be.'

His hands were moving over her body again, stroking, caressing, teasing, and within seconds it was as if the hesitant moment had never been. As if all the past had never been and there was only the two of them, together, lost in their secret sensual world where no one else could ever intrude.

'Don't be afraid. I will show you how this can be. How it should be.'

Fear was the last thing that had a chance to slip into her mind. She was overwhelmed by delight, verging on sensual overload as he seemed to know unerringly how to seek out and find all the tiny pleasure spots that she had never known existed. She felt herself opening up to him, flowering under his caresses. The heated passion that had possessed her from the start was soon blazing wild and fierce again but this time it had a new and deeper urgency, a strength that came from knowing this was truly special, deeply meant.

Their clothes were flung aside, tossed onto the floor in careless impatience and the extra sensitivity born from skin on skin stoked the inner fire, building it higher and higher until she felt that she would surely melt, dissolve away completely in its heat. Where his hands went so did his mouth, kissing a trail of delight that had her writhing under him. She couldn't believe it was possible to feel like this. That a man could make her feel this way.

No, not just any man—Heath.

'Come to me...'

Her hands were clenched over the hard bone and muscles of his shoulders, pulling him down to her in the same moment that she arched up from the bed, capturing his ear lobe in her teeth again and feeling a rush of purely female power as she felt his powerful body buck in heated response.

'Come to me now…I want you.'

'But… Kat…'

For a moment his dark eyes met hers and it seemed that he could actually look into her soul, draw out of her all her most secret thoughts, her deepest longings.

And that was how she wanted it. For the first time she felt she could truly be herself. That whatever was in her spirit, in her soul, the best part of it was the way she felt for this man.

'I'm yours. As you said—I am yours,' she told him and saw his eyes close again, his skin tightened over the strong bones of his face as he swallowed hard.

'You are mine,' he said deeply. 'And I will show you—'

The rest of his words were lost in her uncontrolled cries of pleasure as he set to make good his words, to leave his mark on every part of her body. He reduced her to such a state of sensual abandonment that when he finally brought his powerful body on top of hers, parting her legs with the pressure of one heavy thigh, and pushing close to the pulsing heart of her need, she was already going with him, opening herself to him, urging him on.

But even so, just at the moment of her greatest need, he hesitated just for a second, looked down into her face, stroked strong fingers over her cheek and down into the dark hair spread wild on the pillow around her.

'Ready?'

Unable to find the words to assure him, she let her body speak for her, arching up against him, drawing him to her, taking him in. The sudden sharp, stinging pain took her breath away, stilling him for a moment, but she clung to him hard, holding him still, fearful that he might move away.

'I'm going nowhere,' he muttered in her ear. 'Just tell me—'

'Now...' she cut in on him sharply, almost fiercely as the burn died away and a couple of small, subtle movements relaxed and tantalised her body, woke her hunger all over again, made her yearn for more. 'Oh now!'

Released from any need to hold back, Heath gave her what she wanted. With every slow, powerful thrust he took her further, higher, nearer...until at last she was soaring with him, her head thrown back, her fingers digging into the long hot lines of his back, her legs curling around his waist to deepen every sensation. His name was a litany of delight on her tongue, her body given over completely to delight. To being one with him.

It was wild and it was fierce and strong. It was true to her, to her soul as a woman. It was what she had been born for; why she had lived her life until now. It was what she had been waiting for and what would set her free.

And when the moment of total release came she was swept over the edge into a new and amazing world. A place where sensations she had only ever dreamed of, could barely begin to imagine, bombarded her body and her mind with pleasure that sent her tumbling and spinning into a glorious, golden oblivion.

CHAPTER TEN

MORNING came late after a long sensual night. Exhausted from hours of passionate lovemaking, neither Kat nor Heath stirred until the sun had fully come up, the light of day filling the room.

Kat was the first to wake, yawning and stretching lazily, she felt the pull of muscles she was unaccustomed to having used, the faint bruised feeling between her legs. It was a discomfort she welcomed; the evidence of this new and wonderful stage in her life. She had crossed over into the reality of being totally a woman. A woman with a lover. The man who meant life and joy to her. The man she adored.

Lying beside him, with her elbow propped up on the pillow, she looked down into his stunning face, seeing the way that his long thick black eyelashes fanned out on the olive skin above his cheekbones. Some of his tan had faded over his time in England, but the line of the scar below his eye still showed thin and white after all this time.

Tears burned at the backs of her eyes as she remembered the way that he had come by it and, reaching out a gentle fingertip, she traced the mark softly. The tiny caress broke into the heavy sleep that held him, making his eyelids flicker, the lush lashes fluttering as he stirred slightly.

Bending down, Kat pressed her lips to where her fingers

had just been, wishing she could kiss away the small im-
perfection on his skin. But at the same time she knew
she really couldn't wish it away. It was Heath, as much a
part of him as the colour of his eyes, the way that his hair
peaked at his forehead, his wide, sensual mouth. But she
did wish that she could kiss away the memories of how the
scar had come about, the terrible jealousy that had driven
her brother to hurt him, the bitterness that had driven him
away from her for far too long.

As she lifted her head again she heard his sigh, saw his
dark head stir against the pillow.

'Kat...' Heath said softly and she thought that she could
never, ever tire of hearing her name on his lips.

'I'm so sorry,' she whispered. 'I wish it had all never
happened.'

'Kat...' Heath said again but this time on a very different, very changed intonation. One that had her lifting
her head slightly to see the way that his eyes had opened
fully, heavy lids lifting until he was looking straight into
her eyes.

And the dark depths of his own black gaze seemed like
some bottomless pool into which she might tumble and
drown if she wasn't very careful.

'*Querida...*' he began again, something in the single
word catching on an unexpectedly raw spot in Kat's heart
and giving it a disturbing tug, one that had her frowning
in sudden uncertainty.

'I need to tell you something...' Heath continued but
at that moment there was the sound of a vehicle drawing
to a halt outside, the slam of a car door and a loud ring on
the front door bell.

'Who?'

Already uneasy, Kat found that the noise pushed her
into action before she had time to think, driving her off

the bed and over to the window where she peeped out from behind the curtains, looking down into the drive below. Her heart gave another uncomfortable jolt when she recognised the car, the tall grey-haired man standing on the stone steps.

'Katherine... We need to talk...'

Heath was pulling himself up on the pillows and something in his tone only added to her discomfort, the stream of unease that ran through every nerve. But she wasn't at all ready to consider what might have made him use the full version of her name or put that note into his voice. She felt better able to cope with the one thing she thought she understood.

'It's Randolph—my solicitor. I don't know what he wants but it has to be important.'

She was dashing from the room as she spoke, snatching up underwear and a green tee shirt dress that she could just yank over her head and tug it down to cover her.

'Kat...' Heath's tone was sharper now but she couldn't allow anything to distract her as the doorbell rang again, more loudly this time

'I can't keep him waiting. I have to see him...'

The door slammed behind her as she hurried out. Cursing, Heath flung back the bedclothes and flung himself from the bed, hunting for his clothes in the tangle of discarded garments on the floor.

Not having anything that was as easy to pull on as the dress that Kat had found delayed him for moments he could ill afford to lose and by the time he made it to the bottom of the stairs, still barefooted and fastening the belt around his waist, she had already let the lawyer in and shown him into the sitting room. Through an open door at the far end of the room, the kitchen lights were still burning in spite of the brightness of the day, evidence of how wildly distracted they had been last night.

'Are you sure I can't get you a drink?' Kat was saying, her voice surprisingly calm and collected in spite of the hurried way she had had to gather her thoughts and get down here.

'No, thank you, I'm fine.'

Damn him to hell. If only he could have accepted the drink she offered. That would at least have given him time, a few moments' breathing space to have a quick whispered word with Jordan Randolph, make sure that he was primed, knew exactly what to say. Or—rather—what not to say. Instead he was going to have to rely on facial gestures, signals, in an attempt to get over what he wanted. If only he could get the older man to understand him.

Not that that seemed possible from the way that Randolph responded as soon as he walked into the room.

'Oh, good morning, Senhor Montanha. I didn't expect to see you here yet.'

Kat's expression as she turned to face him was everything he hadn't wanted to see.

'Senhor Montanha? How do you two know each other?'

'We don't.'

But he had spoken too quickly and too sharply. Her frown told him that. And the way that she looked from one to the other, then back to his face where her gaze fixed and held.

'We have never met before.'

Randolph's insertion was perfectly timed, catching Kat's attention. But her frown didn't ease; suspicion still clouded her eyes in her pale face as her fingers tapped restlessly along the back of the settee. Heath suddenly had a searing, vivid memory of her in the bed upstairs, under him, open to him, welcoming him, giving to him. The woman before him looked like a pale copy of that person, and if Randolph blundered any further then everything could blow up in his face.

'I asked to meet him here,' he said now. 'But...'

He turned a disapproving glare on the other man.

'I said ten-thirty.'

'It is ten-thirty—past.' It was Kat who spoke, her tone as stiff as the way she held her slender body as she waved a hand towards the grandfather clock in the corner. 'It's us who's late.'

And he knew why. Already the shadows of regret were creeping into her words. The glorious fulfilment they had shared might as well have seeped out from every pore, soaking into the carpet at her feet, it had vanished so completely. Something that felt like a cruel, cold hand reached inside him and twisted sharply in his guts.

'No problem.'

Jordan Randolph had picked up on the atmosphere—how could he be oblivious to it?—and was hurrying to try and ease the tension.

'I have the whole morning free so don't worry. For something as important as this, I wanted to give you my full attention of course.'

'Of course.'

'As important as what?'

Kat's question clashed with his cynical echoing of that last phrase and Heath knew from the way she was looking at him that he hadn't done a thing to ease her suspicions.

'It isn't—' he began but she cut straight across him.

'Don't tell me what it *isn't*—tell me what it *is*,' Kat said, fighting to force the words past the uncomfortable knots that were tangling in her throat.

After the ecstasies of the night, it seemed that she had woken into a living nightmare, where the passionate ardent

lover Heath had been during the night had become someone else. A man whose face seemed carved from stone and
whose eyes were carefully hooded, hiding every trace of
his thoughts from her.

'Tell me just why my—correction, *Arthur's*—solicitor
is here, when I haven't asked him to come to the Grange
for any reason. And tell me how come he knows who
you are—*Senhor Montanha*—when the only thing that
he and I have ever been involved in is the preparation for
the handover of the Grange and the estate to the Itabira
Corporation. And— Oh, dear God!'

It was as she said the words that the memory came back
to haunt her. The sound of Heath saying, 'An emerald
mine... The Itabira...' And if she had needed any further
proof then the look in his eyes, the way his jaw seemed
to clamp tight over whatever it was he had been about to
say gave her it.

Suddenly she was whirling, facing the man on the settee.

'Mr Randolph...tell me the truth.'

'No...' It was Heath who broke in, his tone coldly unyielding. 'This is between us, Kat. I told you, we had to
talk.'

He walked across to the door, held it open.

'Randolph, I'm afraid you've had a wasted journey. If
you wouldn't mind—I'll take the papers from you now
but I'll call you when I need you again.'

'We don't need to *talk*!' Kat rounded on him almost
before the door had closed behind the lawyer, her eyes
flashing fire. 'No—I'll tell you everything—you listen. I
know what this is all about.'

'You do?' Heath had tossed the documents Randolph
had left onto the sideboard and now he turned to face her.

How could he be so cool, so distant after the night they

had shared? How could he stand there so calmly, hands in pockets, broad shoulders blocking the light from the window, when she felt as if she were splintering into tiny pieces inside? Inside her head it was as if the past couple of months was being replayed, but with a new and terribly distorting emphasis that turned it inside out. And the trouble was that the new focus, the dark and disturbing one, was the truth.

'I do. So let me tell you how it was.'

She almost faltered when he made no reply but simply inclined his head in agreement. Dragging up her strength from somewhere, she faced him and held up her hands, ticking off the points on the fingers of the left with the other.

'One—you always hated Joe—and Arthur—not surprisingly for the way they treated you. Two—you walked out of here all those years ago with a promise that one day you'd be back, and then we'd see. Three—you came back here with scores to settle—you said that quite openly the day you first came here.'

Had he been about to say something? It seemed he had made a move to do so, or at least that there had been some sort of change in his expression. But when she paused, waited, he said nothing. Just stood there, watching her, clearly expecting her to go on.

'Four—you'd already taken possession of High Farm, and everything Joe owned. And five—although I didn't know it—you were moving in on me.'

He'd definitely reacted that time. His head had jerked upward and there had been a flare of—of what? Rejection?—in his eyes. But still he said nothing. He was going to make her say every last appalling thing.

'The Itabira Corporation—*your* corporation—was claiming for the bad debts Arthur had racked up. Unbelievable debts. They were going to take the house—the whole of the estate in payment. All this time I've been dealing with them, Randolph and I have been discussing things with their representatives—*your* representatives. And all this time you have known just what was going on.'

'Yes.'

The first word he had spoken in so long was stark and cold, totally indisputable. But what had she expected? That he would try to deny it? Put some other interpretation on it? What other interpretation was possible?

'You not only knew what was going on but you had planned it, authorised it, put it into action.'

'Yes.'

'You've been playing me all along.'

'No.' It was a very different tone this time. Dark and emphatic, totally rejecting her claim.

'No?'

'I never played you.'

'Of course not,' Kat scorned. 'You knew that your company—that you—were going to take everything I had, but you never said a word. And you don't call that "playing"?'

Now, when the bitterness really hit home, she remembered how on the day they had gone to fetch Harry from school he had asked what she would do with Joe and the little boy now that he owned High Farm. But he hadn't suggested that she bring her brother and nephew to the Grange; hadn't put forward the idea that they could live with her and Isobel.

Because he had already known that the Grange, like High Farm, was his.

'You spent the last weeks working your way into my life—into my trust—and all the time you were instructing your representatives to push for every penny they could get, make sure they left me with nothing. You had me in your power. You let Harry come to—to worship you…'

There was no way she could use the word love even where her nephew was concerned. She was having a hard enough fight to keep it out of her own thoughts. She had lived for just days, a few short weeks, with the knowledge that she loved Heath in her head. She had even, just for a little while, allowed herself to hope that there might be a chance he could come to care for her too. When he had held her after delivering the news of her brother's death, or stood at her side at Joe's funeral, she had let herself believe that he must feel something in order to do that.

She had even… Tears thickened in her throat and had to be swallowed down with a fierce effort. She had even given him herself and her virginity because she had thought that he cared about more than conquering her body. Now it seemed that taking possession—of money— of homes—of *her*—was all that he cared about.

'Not playing? Then what would you call it?'

Heath stirred at last, pushed both his hands through his hair, looked towards the documents on the table, then obviously reconsidered whatever had been going through his mind.

'You think all this was about money?'

The way he had gone onto the attack instead of trying to defend the indefensible was startling, making Kat take a step backwards though he hadn't raised his voice or even darkened it at all.

'It seems the obvious—'

'Obvious? Then if it's so damn apparent that all I wanted was money, tell me why didn't I just come straight out and tell you? Why didn't I let you know that I had you "in my power" if that was what I wanted?'

'Because…because…'

She scrambled about in her thoughts, looking for a reason, but couldn't come up with one. He could have got things his way so much more easily if he had. She didn't want to look too closely at the way her heart lifted in response to that.

'Why didn't you?'

'Because money—or property—doesn't matter. I have more than enough of both. More than any man could want or use in his lifetime. Why should I want more?'

'You said you had scores...'

'Scores to settle, yes. But settling the score with Joe— or your husband—didn't mean making me richer. I wanted them to know what it was like to be in the position I had once been. With no power, no support, no home... And I wanted them to see me in the position they'd once had— the man with the power over them.'

'So you took everything from them.'

Heath lifted one shoulder in a shrug that questioned her assumption.

'Not took. Everything I had I came by legally. Arthur had already made such a mess of his life—he owed more than you could ever imagine. He was involved in some corrupt deals that were meant to ruin one of my companies—instead they ruined him. I took on those debts. I had everything I wanted from him before he died.'

'Then why did you come back?'

Heath moved to sit on the arm of the settee, resting his bare feet on the cushion. The change of position seemed to indicate a change of mood but Kat had no way of knowing just which way his thoughts were heading.

'You know the answer to that.'

'I do?'

Slowly he nodded his dark head, deep, glittering eyes fixed on her face, absorbing her puzzled frown.

'I've answered the question in a different form before now.'

Hunting through her memories wasn't easy with those black eyes fixed on her face, but at last she heard his voice saying *I stayed for you.*

I stayed for you.

He was watching her face more intently now, noting every different nuance of expression that crossed it. And there was something in that scrutiny that made her dig even deeper.

'If—back then—if you stayed for me, then what changed your mind? Why did you leave?'

It was the right question; the change in his expression told her that. Suddenly she knew there was much more to it than the way that he had been treated by her brother.

'I left because of you.'

'Because—what did I do?'

But as soon as she asked the question, she knew the answer. And to her horror she heard Heath quote her own stupid, craven words back at her.

'"Fancy Heath? You have to be joking! I mean—look at him? No money, no job—no class! The Nicholls family may have fallen on hard times, but we do have some pride. How could anyone want him?"'

Her head was spinning. She felt ill at just recalling what she had said.

'You—you heard…'

'I heard.'

But somehow there wasn't the condemnation in his face. Instead there was a sort of understanding.

'I'm so so sorry… I should never…'

What else could she say? She *was* sorry. More so than he could ever imagine.

'Perhaps you should.'

'What?'

Kat couldn't believe she had actually heard right. Had he said . . ?

'Perhaps you should have said those things. Perhaps I should have heard them.'

'No—never!'

'What was happening?' Heath asked quietly and it was the softness in his tone that told her he knew—or guessed. 'Joe—or Arthur?'

'Both.'

She knew he understood now but she still had to say it.

'Arthur was jealous—he'd said that he'd seen you, eyeing me up. He also said that he thought I—I fancied you. Joe was furious when he heard. He said that if any of it was true then he would kill you. That he'd throw you out—no money—no references. And Arthur said that he'd make sure you never got another job anywhere. So I—I...'

'You thought the only way to protect me was to play them at their own game. To tell them that I disgusted you and it would degrade you to have anything to do with me.'

'How did you guess?'

'I didn't—at the time,' Heath admitted, pushing a hand through his hair again. 'At the time I thought that you meant it and I couldn't bear to stay where I wasn't wanted—by you.'

By you. Did that mean as much as she thought it did? She prayed that she wasn't jumping to conclusions.

'I didn't know you were there! I would never...'

'Hey...'

Heath got to his feet and came over to her, bridging the distance between them at last. Standing in front of her, he reached out a hand and brushed the backs of his fingers across her cheeks, bringing them away wet with tears she wasn't even aware that she had shed.

'I understand.'

Sniffing inelegantly, Kat shook her head.

'You shouldn't. You really shouldn't.'

'You were barely fifteen. Your brother was your guardian. Arthur was the local aristocracy while I...You were right, you know.'

'What?' Kat's mouth actually dropped open as she stared up into his dark, handsome, beloved face. 'No...I...'

''Yes,' Heath said firmly, placing a forefinger across her lips to silence her. 'Yes, *querida*. No money, no job—no class—no future—that described me perfectly in those days. It was the wake-up call I needed. I'd told myself I was staying for you—but I wasn't offering you anything worth having if you did turn to me.'

He shook his head as if trying to shake away the memories.

'You gave me a kick to get out of there—make something of myself—make myself a man worthy of you.'

'Worthy!' That made Kat tear her mouth away from the restraint of his hand. 'Oh, Heath—you were always worthy—so much more so than... Oh, dear heaven, what must you have thought when I married Arthur?'

'If I'm honest—I hated you for that. But that was before I took a long hard look at myself and realised that he did have more to offer you than I'd ever had. I hoped he might make you happy. But then I found out about the underhand deals he and Joe were working—and I heard reports about the sort of man Arthur Charlton really was. I planned to come back then but Charlton's downward spiral happened even faster than I'd ever anticipated. Before I could take action he was dead. And no matter what, there was no way I could move in on a newly bereaved widow.'

'I was bereaved long before that,' Kat said softly. 'From

about the first month of my marriage. From the point that
I realised that I never had a husband at all.'

Heath sensed the importance of what she was about to
say. She knew it from the way he went so very still, his
eyes narrowing sharply.

'The reason my marriage to Arthur was never consum-
mated was that he could never get an erection.'

A faint shudder went through her at the memory.

'Oh, it's not that he didn't try but he just couldn't...
The truth is that he was gay. He just wouldn't admit it to
himself. He always used to accuse me—yell at me that it
was my fault. He told me I wasn't sexy—or that...'

'Not sexy...' Heath muttered, shaking his head in disbelief. *'Meu Deus!'*

'He—he said that I was only turned on by a bit of rough.
Like you.'

A rush of shaky, near hysterical laughter shook her and
she reached up a trembling hand to touch his face.

'I think last night...' memories of the glorious, incan-
descent moments in Heath's arms, in his possession, made
her voice shake '...shows he was right. Not that there was
anything *rough* about it. And—Heath...'

She had to tell him this. Wanted him to know it so that
there was no room for doubt in his mind at all.

'The truth is that Arthur never really had a wife—not a
woman who loved him as a wife should. I thought I cared
for Arthur, but deep down I also thought that you were
lost to me. That I would never see you again. And there
was no way that I could want any man the way I wanted
you.'

She saw him close his eyes just briefly and knew that
what she had said had hit home. There was no need to ask
how much it meant to him; it was there in his face, in the

eyes where he wasn't ashamed to let her see the sheen of tears that glistened over them.

She drew in a deep breath, finding within herself the courage to go on. Those tears had given her that.

'So now I'll ask you that question over again—why did you come back?'

'I thought I came back for revenge.' Heath's voice was raw and husky. 'But the truth is that I came back for you because I couldn't forget you, no matter how I tried. I came back for you and if you ask me to—but only if you ask me to—I'll go away again. But first...'

Moving away slightly, he reached for the documents that Randolph had brought. He handed them to her.

'The deeds to the Grange—it's yours. Yours and Harry's. No matter what you decide you'll always have a home and the land and...what the hell...?'

He was staring at her so blankly that she couldn't help but smile. She knew she had done exactly the opposite of what he had thought, but it was the only way she could react.

She had taken the documents in her hand and ripped them in half, then in half again. In the end she let the pieces drop around their feet like rough, oversized confetti.

'I don't want it. I don't want this house—it's Arthur's house—the Charltons' house. I want nothing to do with it. If you want to give it to anyone give it to Isobel.'

'But you—where will you go? You'll need somewhere to live. If you don't want the Grange—then will you take High Farm? I'll have it restored—modernised—turned into the perfect home. I want to give you a home for your future—and Harry's. A place you can make a life. Where you can be happy.'

Kat felt a sob coming into her throat, choking her. He

knew that High Farm had always been home. But without him it had just been a house. No matter how wonderfully it would be restored it would still be nothing more. Desperately she shook her head.

'No?'

'No! I can't accept it—can't you see? I don't want you to go away. And I don't want...' she tried but suddenly his mouth was against hers, his kiss taking the words from her. 'Heath...'

'No—wait—let me say it.'

Looking into the darkness of his eyes, she saw the tiny, flickering flame that had lit up in their depth. The spark of hope that was still so vulnerable he didn't dare speak of it. But he let it show in his eyes.

'Kat—I'm not doing this right—I'm getting things in the wrong order—talking about houses when what I should be saying is will you have me? Will you be my wife—let me love you as I have always wanted to?'

'As you always have,' Kat told him softly, knowing it was the only and absolute truth. 'And that is all I want. I can't be happy if you're not in my life. We're two halves of a whole and I can never be complete without you.'

'So you'll marry me?'

Her kiss, long, deep and passionate and tender, gave him his answer, and she knew from the way he kissed her back that no words were needed. But still she had to say them.

'Yes, my darling, yes. I'll go wherever you are. High Farm—or your home in Brazil...'

'Brazil has never been home,' Heath assured her. 'How can it be when my heart has always been here, with you? And now we can make those two halves into one whole. We'll make a proper home for Harry too, let him grow up in the peace and contentment he needs so much. High

Farm will come alive again. We'll fill the fields with animals, stables with horses—the nursery with the children of our love. It will be our home—our future.'

'A real home.'

Kat cupped Heath's face in both her hands, looked deep into his eyes and saw the glow of true happiness, true contentment, there at last. And knew that in every possible sense of the word he had finally come home at last.

'It will be perfect. How can it be anything else? Anywhere you are will be home for me, because my home—the only place for me—is with the man I love.'

* * * * *

The series you love are now available in

LARGER PRINT!

The books are complete and unabridged—
printed in a larger type size to make it
easier on your eyes.

Harlequin
Romance

From the Heart, For the Heart

Harlequin
INTRIGUE
BREATHTAKING ROMANTIC SUSPENSE

Harlequin
Presents

Seduction and Passion Guaranteed!

Harlequin
Super Romance

Exciting, emotional, unexpected!

Try **LARGER PRINT** today!

Visit: www.ReaderService.com
Call: 1-800-873-8635

Harlequin

A *Romance* FOR EVERY MOOD™

www.ReaderService.com

HLPDIR11

ALWAYS POWERFUL, PASSIONATE AND PROVOCATIVE

⬥ Harlequin®
Desire

Harlequin® Desire delivers
strong heroes, spirited heroines
and compelling love stories.

Harlequin Desire features
your favorite authors, including

ANN MAJOR,
DIANA PALMER,
MAUREEN CHILD
AND BRENDA JACKSON.

Passionate, powerful and provocative
romances *guaranteed!*

For superlative authors, sensual stories
and sexy heroes, choose Harlequin Desire.

⬥ **Harlequin**®

A *Romance* FOR EVERY MOOD™

www.ReaderService.com

HDDIR11

HARLEQUIN® HISTORICAL
Where love is timeless

*Imagine a time of chivalrous knights
and unconventional ladies,
roguish rakes and impetuous heiresses,
rugged cowboys and
spirited frontierswomen—
these rich and vivid tales
will capture your imagination!*

HARLEQUIN HISTORICAL…
THEY'RE TOO GOOD TO MISS!

Harlequin *Super Romance*

...there's more to the story!

Superromance.
A *big* satisfying read about unforgettable
characters. Each month we offer *six* very different
stories that range from family drama to adventure
and mystery, from highly emotional stories to
romantic comedies—and much more! Stories
about people you'll believe in and care about.
Stories too compelling to put down....

Our authors are among today's *best* romance
writers. You'll find familiar names and talented
newcomers. Many of them are award winners—
and you'll see why!

If you want the biggest and best
in romance fiction, you'll get it
from Superromance!

Exciting, Emotional, Unexpected...

Harlequin

A *Romance* FOR EVERY MOOD™